The Lady and the Mountain Fire

The Mountain Series

Book 3

Misty M. Beller

This book is a work of fiction and any resemblance to persons, living or dead, or places, events or locales is purely coincidental. The characters are the product of the author's imagination and used fictitiously.

ISBN: 0-6924319-5-0
ISBN-13: 978-0-6924319-5-5

Dedication

To my Dad.
For your constant support and love.
I will always be grateful for the wisdom, integrity and
work ethic I learned by watching you.
I'm honored to be a Daddy's Girl.

And he said unto me, "My grace is sufficient for thee: for My strength is made perfect in weakness." Most gladly therefore will I rather glory in my infirmities, that the power of Christ may rest upon me.

2 Corinthians 12:9 (KJV)

Chapter One

June 22, 1877
Butte City, Montana Territory

*C*laire Sullivan hated fire, but the magnificence of this flaming sunset took her breath away. Hues of crimson, amber, and magenta lit the evening sky as they outlined the towering peaks of the Rocky Mountains. Such a far cry from the green rolling hills of the North Carolina home she'd left two months ago.

She stood on the front porch of the café where she'd stopped for directions and scanned the area. Everything about this mountain town loomed wild and larger than life. Not just because of the peaks easily seen beyond the buildings on all sides, but also because of the rough-looking men in workers' garb filing in and out of the café door beside her.

Claire inhaled another deep breath. The woman in the café, Aunt Pearl, had said Gram's house stood just two doors down, facing the street behind the little restaurant. Gripping her skirts, Claire gingerly descended the two stairs to the dusty road. She nodded to a man who'd stepped aside, waiting to climb those same steps. "Good evening, sir."

His head bobbed a single nod. Her gaze flicked to his face, then skittered away before he could mistake her for staring. A layer of black soot covered his strong features, and the muscles in his jaw flexed as he waited for her to move out of the way. Claire straightened her shoulders. Apparently, he couldn't be bothered for a simple greeting. Were all the men in Butte so rude?

Following the directions the woman in the café had detailed, Claire found the path that formed a sort of alley behind the buildings and came to the little whitewashed house Gram had described in her letters. Would Gram be home? The trip from North Carolina to the Montana Territory had taken weeks longer than Papa expected. Gram was probably beside herself with worry by now.

Claire swallowed as she rounded the corner of the house and stepped onto the narrow porch lining the front. She ran both hands down her wrinkled, blue traveling suit. She looked so rumpled and stained after five days in that stage coach traveling from Fort Benton, it was a good thing Gram couldn't see her. Claire winced. No, it wasn't a good thing. Losing her eyesight was terrible. If only Gram had been in North Carolina with them, where Papa could have treated her eye disease effectively. He could have made a difference. Not let her go blind like these mining town snake-oil doctors had done.

2

Facing the door with its peeling white paint, Claire raised her fist and knocked. Three solid taps. *Lord, please let her be happy I've come.* She hadn't seen Gram since she was five years old, but reading Gram's letters through the years made Claire feel like she'd talked with her face-to-face. When the last letter had arrived, penned by Gram's neighbor because Gram had lost her sight, Claire's heart had tugged so hard, she couldn't resist. Her grandmother needed help.

Claire glanced at the window to the left of the door. No sounds from inside. Was Gram not home? The steady rhythm of wagons and pedestrians drifted from behind her, the townspeople going about their business. Surely Gram wasn't out there alone. It wasn't safe. How could a blind woman traverse these streets on her own?

Claire knocked again, this time louder. More forceful.

A scream sounded inside. The crashing of metal.

"Gram!" She grabbed the wooden knob on the door and twisted, ramming her hip against the wood to force it open. She needn't have tried so hard. The door swung easily, and Claire stumbled inside, staggering to catch her balance with the force of her charge.

A flash of fire blazed to her left. A tortured moan filled the room as Gram stumbled back from the stove.

Flame leaped at least a foot off the stove's surface.

Claire's mouth went dry, and her feet sank into the wood floors like they were weighted with millstones. She closed her eyes against the images the blaze summoned. She had to think. Had to help Gram. Forcing her eyes open, her gaze darted around the room. What could she use to put it out?

The coffee pot on the back of the stove. *Lord, please let it be full.* Claire used the hem of her skirt to protect her hand as she gripped the handle and dumped the contents over the fire. About a cup of liquid and damp coffee grounds drizzled out, but it was enough to steal the power from the blaze. She smashed the base of the pitcher over the remaining flames again and again until they were nothing but acrid smoke.

"Who? Who is it?" The weak voice from behind jerked Claire's attention.

She spun to find Gram, bent over at the waist and clutching her right hand to her abdomen.

"It's me, Gram. Claire. Are you hurt?" She inched toward her grandmother, then pressed a cautious hand to her shoulder. "Can I see your hand?" Claire slid her fingers down Gram's sleeve and closed on the frail forearm.

"Hurts." Gram's word was more of a gasp as she pulled away from Claire.

"I know. I need to see how badly you're burned. I can help." Gram eased her resistance, and Claire finally pulled the injured hand out where she could get a better view of the palm. Crimson skin peered up at her, mottled in spots by white blisters.

Claire's throat closed as the sight merged into another image, seared into Claire's mind. Huge splotches of deep red covering the young flesh of her childhood friend. She sucked in a breath. Gram wouldn't die from this burn. Not like Mandy. She couldn't.

"Get...water." Gram's voice quavered like it might crack.

"Yes." Claire scanned the room. There was a basin on the counter. She ran to it, dipping her finger in the edge. They needed cold. The water looked relatively clean, but warm from the summer evening. Better than nothing.

"Come sit at the table." She deposited the basin, then gripped Gram's elbow and led her toward the chair.

Gram's milky eyes stared straight ahead as the fingers on her good hand gripped the wood. She eased herself into the chair.

Once Gram was settled with her hand in the basin, Claire stepped back. "Stay here while I get a doctor."

"No need. There's some cream in the bedroom. Just have to wrap it."

Claire's gaze wandered back to the hand in the basin, the seared red palm peeking up from the water. "Gram, this burn is really bad. You need more care than I can give you." Something to ward off infection for sure.

The lines on Gram's forehead deepened. "We don't need to bother them."

"It won't be a bother, Gram. We need medical help." *Lord, please let me find someone competent. Don't let me regret forcing this.* "Stay right here, and I'll be back as soon as I can."

She didn't give Gram a chance to object as she rushed for the door.

When Claire stepped off Gram's porch, she pulled up short. Where to find the doctor? The lady at Aunt Pearl's Café would probably know. Claire hiked her skirts and ran back the way she'd come.

She was panting by the time she charged through the front door of the café. A few people at nearby tables glanced up, but the steady murmur of voices never wavered. Claire searched the faces for the woman she'd spoken to before. Or anyone who looked like they belonged to the establishment. But she found no one.

Skirting the tables, she marched toward a curtain that probably marked the kitchen. As she grabbed the fabric to pull it aside, the cloth jerked from her hand. A woman charged through, and Claire jumped to the side just in time. The look of shock on the woman's face turned to horror as she swayed, twisting to balance a full tray in her left hand and a pitcher in her right. Claire's instincts kicked in, and she reached for the tray. Just in time. Her hands closed on the edges, holding it steady. "Let me have it."

The woman—the one who'd given her directions to Gram's house—eased the tray down as Claire took possession of it.

"If you set it back on my hand, I can balance it. Ye just gave me a fright, is all."

Claire held tight to the wooden sides of the heavy tray. "No, ma'am. I'll carry it to where you need."

The woman's shoulders sagged. "Thank ye, dear. Set it on the corner right here." She motioned toward a table on

6

the second row where two men in rumpled vests and bowler hats had watched their entire exchange.

The woman turned back to her. "Now, can I help ye with somethin'?"

Claire's mind sped. "I need a doctor. My grandmother burned herself. Bad. Can you tell me where the clinic is?"

Aunt Pearl twisted to eye Claire as she poured coffee into a mug for one of the bowler hat men. "You're in luck. Doc Bryan's right here."

Where? Claire glanced at the men under the hats. The one facing her had a mustache that hung over the corners of his mouth like the roof on a house, making his face look especially long. Was he the doctor?

"Doc Bryan, this is Alice Malmgren's granddaughter. She's aneedin' ya." The long-faced man didn't look up at Aunt Pearl's words.

A wave of the woman's hand brought Claire's attention to the table beside them. A soot-covered man wiped his fingers with a cloth and stood, scooting his chair back with a single fluid motion.

He was a doctor? Claire squinted at him. The man she'd met by the café stairs after her first visit. The one who couldn't be bothered to speak a greeting.

"Doc Bryan's the best you'll find anywhere." Aunt Pearl patted his shoulder like a doting mother.

Claire cringed at the black grime that must surely be on the woman's hand now. Could she trust this ruffian? Perhaps she could find an apothecary and treat Gram herself?

Too late. The man moved to the aisle, a black physician bag in his hand. His shoulders sagged, as though the case weighed a hundred pounds. He raised his eyes to hers, their brown depths surprisingly clear. He wasn't as old as she'd first thought. Thirty, perhaps. Maybe less than that, though who could tell under the grime.

"Is she at home?"

The doctor's voice shook Claire from her thoughts. "Yes, follow me." She charged forward and slipped past him.

"I know where she lives." The sardonic tone in his voice caught her up short. Claire twisted to peer at him. Did his rudeness have no bounds? He strode close behind her. He might run her over if she didn't get out of the way. Claire squared her shoulders and strode toward the café exit.

She had to half-jog to Gram's to keep up with the man's long strides. He didn't seem to be trying to leave her behind. Just going about his business without regard to her or anything else besides his purpose. *Lord, please let his doctoring skills be better than his bedside manner.*

At the very least, she'd get salve and bandages from him and care for Gram herself. Heaven knew she'd wrapped her share of injuries when she made house calls with Papa.

With only a quick tap on the door, the *doctor* twisted the handle and pushed inside. Claire stopped to catch her breath on the threshold as she watched him scan the room.

He strode toward a washstand at the end of the worktable.

Claire moved to Gram's side and watched as he scrubbed his hands, bits of gray lather flicking onto the counter.

After he'd dried them on the cloth, he stepped to the table and knelt by Gram's side. He murmured something Claire couldn't hear as he reached for the burned hand and pulled it from the water to examine.

"Silly me," Gram said. "I touched the stove top when I knew better." The lines on her face folded to a grimace as he fingered the fiery red skin. "Oh," she hissed.

Claire stepped closer. "Don't make it worse. Be careful with her." Her fingers itched to jerk the man back. She gripped them in fists to fight the urge. For now.

"When you do something," the doctor said, "you don't go halfway, do ya?" He kept his focus on Gram as his deep voice rumbled. He rested her hand palm-up on the table while he dug for something in his bag. There was a hint of a brogue in his tone. Maybe Irish?

He pulled out a small bottle, removed the cork, and placed the glass in Gram's good hand. "Take a little swig of this, and you'll feel better."

"What are you giving her?" Before Claire could stop her, Gram obeyed.

At last, the doctor applied salve and wrapped the palm with a long bandage. Claire caught a quick glimpse of discolored spots on the angry red skin before she pinched her eyes shut against the sight. But the images in her mind were worse. Seared flesh, burns so deep they looked almost purple.

Spinning around, she forced her eyelids open and stared out the window. Anything to distract herself. A woman trudged down the street, one hand holding a basket, the other clutching the wrist of a red-haired boy. A swelling in the woman's abdomen signaled the pending arrival of a new sibling within a few months. Would it be a brother or sister to the child?

"There now," the doctor said. "A few days with that on, and you'll be good as new."

Claire spun at his words. He'd worked in silence until now. Not a very talkative chap, was he?

"Thank ye, Bryan. I'm feeling better already." Gram patted his shoulder with her good hand.

Claire cringed. What was it with ladies touching this man's dirty shoulder? Of course, Gram had no way of seeing how filthy he was.

Even though he'd washed his hands, his face could use a good scrubbing. And his clothes? It'd take two tubs of water to get them clean.

"You can finish washing up while I help Gram to bed." No sense in giving him an option in the matter.

He only nodded as he closed the leather case and stood. His knees cracked like an old man's. Maybe he wasn't any younger than thirty. Claire bit back a smirk at the frightfully unkind thought. *Sorry, Lord.*

Bryan Donaghue scrubbed the soap over his cheeks and forehead, closing his eyes as much to enjoy the clean lye scent as to keep out water. Too bad he couldn't dunk his entire head in the little tin wash basin. What he wouldn't do for a big tub of warm water in front of the cook stove like Mum used to prepare when they were kids.

With the suds rinsed off, Bryan eyed the stained white cloth on the counter. Had he left those gray smears when he'd washed earlier? How much more damage would he do now? This dust from the mine was like a plague, infecting everything within reach. He ignored the cloth and scrubbed a palm down his face, then shook his hands dry.

He turned to lean against the ledge while he waited for Mrs. Malmgren's pretty visitor to come out of the sleeping chamber. News of her arrival hadn't reached him before tonight, although Mrs. Malmgren had chattered about her coming for months. The feisty older woman got around pretty well without her sight, but it was a good thing family finally came to help her. What took them so long?

Of course, the snooty lady hadn't done such a great job keeping her grandmother safe so far. She may be a pretty thing, but she'd do better to help her grandmother instead of being rude to people who were trying to do that very thing.

He glanced around the dingy room. When had she arrived? It must not have been long ago. Either that or she could do a better job of cleaning, too.

Bryan forced out a long sigh. That wasn't fair. She'd traveled thousands of mile to help her grandmother. He was just so blasted tired, he couldn't think straight.

He crossed his arms and allowed his chin to drop to his chest. Every bone and muscle in his body ached. He'd spent most of the afternoon at the Travona mine, helping pull timbers off trapped workers after a nitroglycerine explosion blew too early. Several broken limbs, but no deaths. This time. How many would die in the next explosion? He had to stop the dangerous conditions before it was too late.

He inhaled a deep breath, then released it slowly, allowing his lungs and shoulders to collapse. After pulling injured people from the mine and stitching their wounds, he didn't have it in him to offer hospitality to a newcomer in town. He'd have to make it up to her later.

"How much do we owe for your services?"

He jerked his head up at the snippy female voice. The woman seemed a bit low on good manners herself. Was that what all people were like back in…where was she from? South Carolina?

Bryan pushed away from the work counter. "I'll add it to her tab. Your grandmother pays at the end of the month." He scooped up his case and headed for the door.

"Can I...offer you coffee or"—she gazed around the messy kitchen, seemed to falter—"or something before you go?"

Bryan slowed as he neared the door and turned. "Don't bother. Pearl will have my food saved at the café."

"Suit yourself."

Ouch. He hadn't meant his words to come out so short, but she didn't have to be rude. Why was he letting her rile him? With a flick of his glance, he took in the room. "You might want to clean up around here. If her burned skin gets dirty, she could lose the hand from infection." He gave what he hoped was a polite nod, yanked the door open, and strode outside.

Sleep. He'd apologize after some sleep. But for now, it took every ounce of his self-control not to slam the door behind him.

Chapter Two

Claire clasped her hands and leaned into the stretch, bending sideways to avoid bumping into the wall at the head of the bed. One by one, each of the muscles in her shoulders and neck pulled out their kinks from yesterday's long stage ride to Butte City. What an evening it had been, finding Gram with her hand so badly burned. Then the run-in with that sullen doctor. He may be handsome—in a rugged mountain sort of way—but he could certainly do some studying in the arts of kindness and sympathy. And cleanliness.

How would Gram feel this morning? She sat up in bed. Gram. Claire patted the blanket beside her. Empty. Her chest pounded. How had Gram gotten up without her waking?

Throwing the covers aside, Claire swung her feet to the floor. The coolness of the wood made her toes curl. "Gram?" Darkness swallowed the windowless bedroom. Had she overslept? She pulled the latch on the door and crept into the main room of the small house. "Gram?" No movement. No sound.

God, please don't let me lose her already. Claire scurried through the room to the front door. Maybe Gram had gone to use the outhouse they shared with the residence next door.

Claire stepped onto the porch and stopped short at the figure in the rocking chair to her left.

"Clara Lee?"

Claire pressed a hand to her chest, exhaling a long breath. "Gram. You gave me a start."

A smile tipped the corners of the older woman's mouth as her unseeing eyes faced the distance. "Thought I'd wandered off and got lost, did you?"

Good thing Gram couldn't see the heat radiating from her face. Claire stepped over and sank into the matching rocker beside Gram. "I didn't realize I'd overslept so much."

Gram motioned toward the view in front of them. "I try to be up for the sunrise every mornin', and visit with the Lord."

Claire took in the distant horizon. Brilliant ambers, pinks, and indigos melded together where the sky met the mountain peaks. The summits were shadowed on some sides, while other sections radiated the reflection of the dazzling sky. "Oh my." Such paltry words for the magnificence before them.

"I told your grandpop it didn't matter where he built our home, just so long as I could see the sun rise over the mountains each mornin'. He always said every day's a new beginning." Gram's voice quivered with memory.

Claire glanced over and smiled. A glimpse of Gram's milky eyes brought reality into clear focus. Gram couldn't see this sunrise. Wouldn't see any more of these spectacular starts to the day. She reached over and grasped the wrinkled hand.

Gram seemed to read her thoughts. "God's given me so many wonderful memories, Clara Lee. Now it's my time to bless Him back. Sometimes I think I'd get so caught up in the beauty of the sunrise, I'd forget about the One who made it for me. Now, my focus is on Him."

The leathery hand squeezed around Claire's fingers, and Claire fought down the knot in her throat. What a special woman her grandmother was.

After a while, Claire pushed to her feet. "I suppose I'll get started on breakfast."

Gram patted her arm as she walked by. "I usually have toast and an egg, darlin', but fix whatever you like."

"That sounds fine." Claire cringed as she stepped into the house. She couldn't let Gram know how hard that simple request would be. Eyeing the cook stove that had been the scene of so much turmoil the night before, she forced herself toward it. Would there be enough coals left so she could just add wood? *Lord, please let there be coals. Give me strength.* She'd known she wouldn't always have Mama to tend the fire, and the day had come. She could do this.

The stove door was warm to the touch. A good sign, but it still raised bumps over Claire's arms. Several white coals sat in a cluster inside the fire box, and Claire exhaled a shaky breath. *Thank you, Lord.*

Beside the stove lay a stack of split wood, and next to it, a smaller pile of kindling. Who kept Gram supplied in wood? She must pay a lad to help, for how could Gram possibly manage this herself? At home, Papa bartered services with a family down the road. Ready firewood in exchange for the medicine their son needed to quell his breathing episodes.

As Claire loaded the small strips of wood into the firebox, she steeled herself against the red glow of the embers coming to life. She had to overcome this fear. Today. It couldn't cripple her any longer. She had work today and people to help. Namely, Gram.

The embers flickered into flame, and Claire closed the iron door against the red glow. At least it was started now, and she could focus on a more pleasant task. Cooking.

After a simple breakfast of eggs and toast, Claire unwrapped Gram's burned hand, applied the salve the doctor had left, and redressed the wound. Gram kept her mind distracted from the obvious pain by prattling on about how wonderful Doc Bryan and his younger brother Doc Alex were. How Alex finally got smart and married up with a sweet little mountain gal who fit him "better 'an two chicks in the same egg."

"It's special when ye find the man God made fer ya, Clara Lee. More than special." She patted Claire's cheek as Claire tied the loose ends of the bandage in place. "When ye find him, don't waste time. Treasure every moment God gives ye."

Before Claire could decide how to answer, Gram sat up straighter. "Well, best we start on the bread for today. I'm gettin' a late beginnin', but with the two of us, we'll make quick work of it."

"Bread?" Her mind stumbled over the sudden change in topic.

Gram rose and shuffled to the work counter, then groped along until she found her apron. "Yep, I bake a dozen loaves each mornin' fer Pearl to use in the café. She's got her hands full, what with her niece leavin' town. The money she pays helps cover expenses around here."

Claire glanced around the room. It was small and sparse, only slightly larger than their kitchen back home. The work counter, washbasin, and cook stove spanned one wall, and the table and four chairs held the center of the room. A pair of upholstered chairs on the opposite wall served as the remaining furniture. The floral pattern on the seats and backs looked worn and a little shredded, most likely due to many long evenings passed there. She could picture Gram in one, her hands busy with needlework. Claire had only met Grandpop once when she was five, but could envision him now with white hair and wire spectacles as he read to Gram.

A clatter behind jerked her from the happy scene. She whirled to see Gram unfolding a flour sack. A tin bowl sat on the counter beside her with a spoon handle sticking out. That must have been the clang. "Let me help you with that,

Gram." She strode to her grandmother's side and pulled the sack closer so they could both reach it. "You tell me how much to measure out and I'll do it for you."

Gram's good hand settled over one of Claire's. "Darlin', there's nothin' I'd like more than fer you to work in the kitchen with me. But you don't have to do things for me. Work alongside."

"But your hand…" Claire's lower lip found its way between her teeth. "Sorry. What can I do?"

"How about you stoke the fire so it'll be ready. Then you can measure out the sourdough starter. I always make a mess o' that gooey stuff."

The fire. She had to overcome this. Claire moved to the fire, picked up a decent sized log, opened the door to the fire box, and closed her eyes as she shoved the wood inside. There. Claire dusted her hands and turned to work on the bread.

They settled into a comfortable rhythm, and by the time Claire pulled the eleventh and twelfth loaves from the oven, her feet ached from standing so long. But they'd really accomplished something. As she set the steaming fare out to cool, Gram finished wiping off the work counter, shook the crumbs into the scrap bucket, then draped the cloth over a hook.

"What say we sit and rest?" Claire picked up the list she'd been making of supplies they needed. "Can I refill your coffee?"

"Thank ye, dear. That'd be nice."

Claire filled her own mug, too, but frowned at the stuff. Cool milk would be nice right now. Maybe she could add it to her notes.

While Gram nursed her brew, Claire recounted the items she'd scratched on the paper. "I have sugar, potatoes and lard. Thought I'd get milk, too. Are there other staples we need for meals? Beans? Beef?"

She glanced up to see Gram shaking her head. "Put the baking supplies on the café's tab. I have enough of the rest. Get a pint of milk for yourself, but none for me."

Focusing her gaze on Gram, Claire absorbed the words. "You don't like milk?"

Gram's mouth pinched. "No, honey. Coffee's fine for me. I don't need it as rich as this, either."

Something didn't smell right here. She'd take a good inventory of the shelves before she left. "So when should I take the bread to Miss Pearl's?"

One side of Gram's mouth tipped up. "You'd best call her Aunt Pearl. She's not been a 'Miss' for many a year, but she won't talk about the Mister. She'll be expectin' ya soon. She'll be even happier if you're early, so she don't have to worry 'bout the bread comin'."

"Would you like to walk with me?" Claire examined her grandmother as she debated the wisdom of the offering. Gram's shoulders stooped as she leaned both elbows on the table.

"Believe I'll let you enjoy the town on yer own this time." Gram stifled a yawn. "Me old bones would do well with a nap before we start bakin' the pies for tonight."

Claire's brows rose as her stomach tumbled. "Pies?"

Gram's smile was thinner than it had been that morning. "Yes, Clara Lee. I make the bread for lunch and somethin' sweet for after dinner."

Poor Gram was working herself into an early grave.

After Claire helped Gram to bed and sorted through the foodstuffs, the inventory of needed supplies grew into a lengthy list. Was money a problem? Or simply the challenge in getting to the store?

Claire removed her apron and swiped a hand to straighten her skirt. No matter the reason, Gram wouldn't go without again. Not as long as Claire Sullivan was here to help.

Aunt Pearl did seem thankful to have the bread before the lunch rush started. She flitted about the kitchen like a whirlwind. Claire hated to make her stop so she could ask for directions to the mercantile.

Aunt Pearl didn't stand still though. While pulling a tray of chicken pies from the oven, she rattled off the two turns and street names.

"Thank you, ma'am." Claire backed from the room.

Aunt Pearl glanced up with a nod, then turned back to stir the gravy on the stove.

Lanyard's Dry Goods turned out to be larger than Claire expected for the rustic town. With a long picture window on either side of the door, it spanned half a block. How hard must it be to get glass all the way to Montana, especially considering the week of travel in the back of a wagon traversing the mountain country.

She stepped through the front door, but no bell announced her presence like the mercantile back home. Perhaps that was too much trouble to ship. She bit back a grin.

So many familiar smells rushed at her in the densely packed store, Claire paused at the head of an aisle to savor them. Leather. Wood. A dusty whiff like quilts long stored in a trunk.

"Can I help you, ma'am?"

Claire jerked her eyelids open and glanced around for the source of the voice. A man stood behind the tall counter. About her age with a trim red mustache, freckles stood out against his pale skin.

"Um, yes." She squared her shoulders and stepped to the counter, pulling the list from her skirt pocket. "I need to have these items delivered to my grandmother's house. Mrs. Alice Malmgren on Ottawa Street." Holding the paper so he could see, she pointed to some of the entries. "The supplies I underlined will be used for Aunt Pearl's Café, and should be charged to her account. The remainder should be posted to my grandmother's tab. I imagine you're familiar with that arrangement?"

She paused to take a breath, her heart beating a rapid staccato. Would he think it strange for her to be purchasing items against the café's account? Shouldn't she need some kind of written authorization for that? This man didn't know her from Queen Elizabeth.

His orange brows knit as he studied the list. Then without meeting her gaze, he turned toward a doorway behind him. "Just a second, ma'am."

Claire laced her fingers together. Did that mean he was gathering the supplies? Shouldn't he have more questions for her? Should she stand here and wait? She'd caught a glimpse of bolt goods on a long table and would love to examine the fabrics. Maybe they'd have some material she could use to recover Gram's chairs. And wouldn't new curtains do wonders to cheer up the place? A yellow floral would be nice and pleasant.

Just as Claire turned that direction, the door through which the clerk had disappeared opened again. She swiveled back. A tall, brawny man with a dark mustache and sideburns appeared, sleeves rolled to reveal sinewy muscles. The apron he wore did nothing to soften his toughness. He caught her gaze with raised brows. "Mrs. Malmgren's granddaughter?"

"Yes." Claire stepped forward and dipped a quick curtsy. "Miss Claire Sullivan."

His mouth pinched into a thin line. "I'm Bob Lanyard." He glanced down at the paper between his fingers. Her list. "I'm afraid we can't fill everything on here. We'll send the stuff for Pearl of course, but…" He raised his gaze to meet hers squarely. "Your grandmother has quite a tab here."

Claire swallowed, but it did nothing to quiet her racing heart. Still, she didn't drop her gaze. "How much?"

"Almost thirty dollars."

She fought to keep from coughing as the sum registered. *Thirty?* That was a month's wages for some men. How could Gram possibly rack up that much? Didn't she pay on the account at all? And how could this man allow it?

"Sir, I…" She struggled to find the question to ask first. "How… I mean, does she…?"

His face flicked a glimpse of sympathy. "We know things are hard on her, so I let her get the basic necessities. She comes and pays every week with what she makes from Pearl." A bit of steel crept back over his features. "Things cost a lot up here."

That was probably true, but thirty dollars? Claire inhaled a breath, then let it leak slowly. "Okay. Let's do the items for the café, the beans, and half the beef." She reached into her pocket for the five dollars she'd brought along just in case. It was all of her spending money, but she could part with a little for Gram. "How much will that be?"

"Two-fifty." He didn't move. Was he waiting for her to pay before he'd even package the stuff?

He must not have understood her. "What about for just the beans and meat? The remainder should go on Aunt

Pearl's tab." She tried to keep a pleasant tone. No need to make the man feel dumb.

"Two fifty for the beans and meat." His dark brows rose a fraction, as if daring her to question him again.

Claire fought the urge to drop her jaw. This man was taking advantage. Fire stirred in her gut, spreading through her veins. She hated bullies. Forcing herself to breathe deeply, she focused on the list in the man's hand while her mind whirled. Gram had said this was the best place to shop. Of course, Gram didn't know the man was fleecing her for every half-penny he could get.

She could go ahead and purchase the supplies for the café's baked goods, then shop elsewhere for their own food. But she needed to get back to help Gram with the pies. And maybe she wouldn't have time to find another mercantile today. Gram's coffers were very close to empty, and they'd need something to eat tonight and tomorrow until she could get to another store.

Eyeing the man again, she spoke through gritted teeth. "I'll take the supplies underlined for the café, and half the amount of beans. How much will that be?"

He glanced at the list again. "Seventy-five cents."

She couldn't hold in the explosion any longer. "Seventy-five cents for a half sack of beans?"

His gaze locked with hers again and never wavered. "We get the beef local. The beans have to be imported from Illinois."

"I'll take the beef then." And he'd be lucky if she didn't beat him with it.

The man shrugged. "Fifty cents."

Chapter Three

*G*ram stirred in her chair when Claire stepped into the little house.

"There's my Clara Lee. I was about to start the vinegar pies."

The weight of Claire's ire with that bully of a storekeeper slid away at the sight of Gram, hair protruding at angles where she'd slept on it, and wrinkles of love caressing her face.

"Are you feeling better then?" She set the supplies on the work counter.

"Like a six week old kitten."

The image forced a smile onto Claire's face. "So glad to hear it."

She held back as Gram gathered ingredients for the crust and floured the rolling surface. It was amazing how well Gram maneuvered using her delicate sense of touch. Each movement so patient until she had the object exactly as she wanted. While Gram kneaded and rolled out the pie

27

crusts, Claire measured out ingredients for the filling. "How many did you say we're making?"

"Eighteen. Been making fifteen pies each night, but Pearl said she's runnin' short, so I said I'd make more. Those men get awful cranky when ya deny 'em somethin' sweet."

Eighteen pies. "I don't know how you do it, Gram."

Gram chuckled. "Sure puts Bill Lanyard on his toes keepin' up with my supplies."

All trace of a smile left Claire's mouth as she thought about that oversized shyster. Thirty dollars. How were they ever to repay such a sum? "Gram, how much does Aunt Pearl pay you for the baking?"

"Fifty cents a day. An' that's just for my time. She provides the foodstuffs."

So Gram had to work for three days just to buy a bag of beans. And if she worked every day of the week, she'd only earn…fifteen dollars in a month. Claire inhaled a deep breath. How could they ever repay the bill at Lanyard's store? Maybe she could negotiate with him to settle for a lower cost? After all, his prices were nothing short of robbery. But could they even pay half that sum?

No. The problem wasn't Gram spending too lavishly for her wages. The problem was nowhere near enough income.

"What's wrong, Clara Lee?" Gram's voice quivered with love.

Her chest squeezed. Gram and her brother Marcus were the only people who'd gotten away with calling her Clara Lee since she was five years old. In school, she'd hated

28

the nickname. But the way Gram said it was special. "Gram, are there any respectable jobs for women here?"

Gram's shoulders stiffened. "Yer lookin' for a job?"

"Just to earn some spending money, help pay my way." The last thing she wanted was for Gram to think she didn't want to spend time with her. "The trip out here cost more than Papa expected, so I'm almost out of spending money. Not a long job, just a few hours a day while you're napping or something." She had to stop for a breath.

A smile played at the corners of Gram's mouth. "It's okay, Clara Lee. I understand you need a little somethin' of your own to do while you're here. And I like that yer a hard worker."

Claire let out a long breath. Gram's mouth puckered in a thoughtful pose, so she stayed quiet.

At last, Gram said, "You should check with Aunt Pearl. She's been in sore need of help since her niece married up with a rancher and moved up the mountain. She'd probably be more tickled than a robin with a worm to have you."

Four hours and eighteen pies later, Claire stood at the back door of the café with two crates stacked on top of each other. A faint aroma of vinegar mixed with the savory smells already had her stomach growling.

The door opened to her knock, and a black-haired woman Claire hadn't seen before stood with a spoon in one hand. A motion at the base of the woman's skirts caught Claire's attention. A toddler peeked from behind the fabric, her curls as dark as her mother's and a fist covering her mouth as she sucked a thumb.

Claire blinked. Had she come to the right door?

The woman turned away to stir a pot on the stove, the child trailing behind her with a hand clutching skirts. "Put them on the table, please."

The woman's voice was so soft, Claire wouldn't have understood the words if they hadn't been so carefully enunciated. Obeying, she placed the crates on the long, sturdy table in the center of the kitchen. "Do you want me to take the pies out of the boxes?"

"Yes, thank you." The woman's speech was so proper, and a little formal. But something about her cadence had an exotic lilt. She didn't glance at Claire again, but spooned a creamy, lumpy substance onto plate after plate. Dumplings? The aroma filling the room brought a gurgle to Claire's stomach.

A noise behind grabbed her attention, and Aunt Pearl bustled into the room, an empty tray in hand. She didn't seem to notice Claire's appearance as she strode to the counter beside the other woman and began loading plates on the tray. "How'do, Miss Sullivan. Hope your grandma's feelin' better. T'was good timing of you ta come when ya did."

"Yes, ma'am." With both women's backs facing her, she might as well have been talking to herself. "She seems much better today. We made eighteen vinegar pies like she said you'd asked."

"We'll need ever' one of 'em. Crowd's started early tonight." With the tray loaded, Aunt Pearl hoisted it to her shoulder and turned toward the cloth separating the dining room.

This was her chance. Claire's heart raced as she stepped toward the older woman. "Aunt Pearl?"

The tray paused and the lady sent an impatient glance. "Can ya walk an' talk? Got a hungry group."

And that was all the pause Claire got. She scrambled to catch up, ducking through the cloth as it swayed in Pearl's wake. "Aunt Pearl, I was wondering if you'd be interested in hiring me for a few hours a day. I can help cook or serve, either one. I'm capable in the kitchen." Claire worked to breathe and walk as she lengthened her stride to stay in hearing range of the woman.

She almost plowed into her when Aunt Pearl stopped at a table and lowered her tray to the wooden surface. Aunt Pearl shot Claire a glance but didn't answer as she handed out the plates to the six men eating family style at the long table. She responded with a nod to the thankful words from the diners, then picked up the empty tray and headed back toward the kitchen with undivided focus. "I'd be glad to have you. Need a server more'n I need those toes I lost to frostbite in '62. Can ye start now?"

"Now?" Feet already aching, Claire double-stepped to keep up. "I, um… I guess." Her mind raced to catch up with the offer. "I need to tell Gram I'll be gone for a few hours. Is that okay?"

Aunt Pearl stopped then and turned to face Claire squarely, her faded brown eyes locking with Claire's. "Do what you need to. We work hard here, but I pay a decent wage. A dollar fifty for workin' lunch and dinner, same as Lilly. I won't babysit ya, but you tell me if you've a problem an' I'll make it right. Sound fair?"

Claire let out a breath. "Perfectly. I'll be back soon, ready to work."

Bryan paused on the front porch of the café and pulled off his cap to run a hand through his hair. No billow of dust or soot today. Staying clean from mine dust was one more benefit to days like this, when he rode into the mountains for house calls to the ranchers. He pulled open the solid wood door. A downside, though, was the late hour he usually returned. Would Aunt Pearl have anything but scraps left? Certainly nothing sweet by this time. A sigh escaped him. Third night this week he'd been too late for Mrs. Malmgren's pies.

The dining area held only a few stragglers. Martin Daly, owner of The Alice mine, sat with Harris, one of his superintendents. The blacksmith and his wife hunkered at a small table by the wall.

Aunt Pearl swept through the back curtain, rag in hand. She waved when she saw him, and veered to a nearby table to scoop up a coffee pot. "Have a seat, Doc. It's chicken an' dumplin's tonight. We'll get a plate out directly."

He settled into a chair near the back wall, so she wouldn't have to walk as far. Pearl poured dark brew into his tin mug. "You let me know if this t'ain't warm enough. Got a slice of vinegar pie left, too, I think."

He managed a thankful smile at those words, even though his weary muscles objected.

She bustled back toward the kitchen and stuck her head around the curtain, spoke a few muffled words to the kitchen staff, and then proceeded to wipe down one of the longer tables.

Bryan draped his arms on his table and allowed his head to drop so his forehead rested on the wooden edge. The pull in his neck muscles stretched out kinks that had built from hours of riding Cloud up the mountain trails. He should have gone back to his room off the clinic and not bothered Aunt Pearl for dinner this late. Alex and Miriam had said he could stop by their new little house any time for a meal. But they were still newlyweds, even though they'd been married six months. It never failed at some point during the meal, they'd look at each other with lop-sided, sappy-eyed smiles. No better way to make a fellow feel like he didn't belong. Yep, once a week was plenty to bother them for dinner.

Normally the quiet in the clinic at night didn't trouble him. Most times it was his solace. But tonight the thought had been unbearable.

So...here he sat, one of the last lonely souls at Aunt Pearl's. He should take the time to filter through his recent patients. Make a mental list of those he needed to follow up on. Wonder how Mrs. Malmgren's burned hand was healing? An image of her snappy granddaughter flashed through his mind. She'd said her last name was Sullivan, so was she Irish? In the light from the lantern, her hair had glistened a russet auburn, a bit more brown than his. But those dark eyes. Those weren't Irish. They were bewitching.

Footsteps sounded and Bryan lifted his head. That pair of captivating dark eyes stood beside his table, holding a plate piled high, a pert set to her full lips.

He blinked. Was this a dream? Had he summoned her with his thoughts?

"Your dinner, Doctor?" She set the plate on the table where he leaned, and Bryan jerked back, his eyes tracking the plate as she slid it in front of him. The aroma of this food sure made it seem like he was awake, but why was *she* bringing it to him at the café?

He raised his gaze back to those enchanting eyes. "What are you doing here?"

Her brows rose. "Serving you dinner. Did I leave out something you need? Perhaps a little sugar to soften you up?" The challenge in her stare was unmistakable.

He dropped his gaze to the food. Maybe his question had come out a bit more direct than it should have, but he was too tired to prance around what he meant. She didn't have to be such a snob about it, though. "Food's fine."

As he fingered his fork, her presence still loomed beside the table like an evening shadow. Should he say something else? Ah, yes. Glancing up, he forced himself not to focus on those sparking eyes. "How's Mrs. Malmgren's burn?"

A look flashed across her face, but he couldn't catch its meaning. "Fine."

So she wanted to play that game, did she? Why couldn't they just have a civil conversation? He focused on his food and loaded a dumpling on his fork. "Bring her to the clinic tomorrow so Alex can check it. If there's infection, we need to catch it early."

The shadow over him stiffened, but he kept his focus on his plate. After a few seconds, the silhouette slid away, and fading footsteps sounded her departure. Bryan couldn't stop himself from watching the woman stalk back toward the kitchen. Why couldn't he keep a gracious tongue when she was around? He'd have to do something to make it up to her. But what?

Claire whipped the cloth aside and stomped to the bucket of wash water in the dry sink. Who did that sham doctor think he was? As if she couldn't see if there was a problem with Gram's hand. And would it have hurt him to keep a civil tone? He minced words like he was paid extra for rudeness.

She sank her hands into the water and found the wash rag. *God, I'm trying to be kind here, but something about him rubs me wrong. Help me show him Your love even when he's rude.*

Her pulse slowed as she rubbed the cloth over a soiled plate and allowed God's grace to sink over her. *With Your strength, Lord.*

Chapter Four

*W*ith her new job, it was two days before Claire found an opportunity to walk with Gram to the clinic to have her hand checked. The wound didn't seem to have healed much. So she'd made time this afternoon, preparing the cherry tarts when they'd baked the bread that morning. When they returned from the clinic, they'd only need to stoke the fire and put the tarts in the oven.

The fire. She'd been doing better with it these last two days. The flashbacks no longer came as long as she looked away from the flame.

Gram pushed open the clinic door, and Claire followed her through, then scanned the little waiting room. Not very different from Papa's back home. She soaked in the familiar smells. Antiseptic. Something tangy like an herb.

"We'll sit until the Doc's ready for us." Gram used her cane to feel the way to a nearby waiting chair. She must have come here a lot to be so familiar with the layout of the room. And how did she know the doctor wasn't ready?

Gram seemed clear on what she was doing, though, so Claire lowered herself in the chair beside her. The room was cleaner than she'd expected for a little mountain clinic, and pretty green calico curtains draped the front window.

A male voice murmured in another room, then grew louder as a door opened in the hallway. "Send your husband for one of us when the time comes."

That voice. Claire strained to hear. Could the brothers sound so similar?

"Thank you, Doc Bryan. I hope it's soon."

No. The woman's words struck like a bell clanging in Claire's ears. Wasn't the other brother supposed to man the clinic? Why was this ill-mannered doctor here today of all days?

She couldn't look at him. Even as Gram shuffled beside her and rose to her feet. The sound of the front door opening, then closing, echoed through the room.

"Mrs. Malmgren." The doctor's voice held more warmth than usual. Maybe he was in his "doctoring" mode and wouldn't be as rude. "Good to see you again."

Holding in a sigh, Claire pushed to her feet and turned to slip Gram's hand onto her arm.

The doctor gave her a cursory nod. "Miss Sullivan." Then he spun and strode down the hallway. Did he expect them to follow? Claire gritted her teeth.

Inside the little exam room, the well-known smells grew even stronger. Claire inhaled a breath. Gram patted her arm. "Smell familiar?"

Out of the corner of her eye, she saw the doctor glance at her. Claire ignored him and leaned close to answer Gram. "I wonder how Papa's doing? Mama said she would help him while I'm gone."

A smile found its way to Gram's face. "My daughter's a saint."

The weight of Doc Bryan's gaze seemed to grow stronger. Why was he staring? Concerned now that he knew she had a little experience with medicine? Maybe he was worried she'd see right through his quackery. She turned to meet his gaze squarely, her eyes narrowing. Let him worry.

His expression changed, and he turned to Gram. "Please, have a seat Mrs. Malmgren. Did you come in for a check on your hand?"

"Yep. Claire's been tellin' me fer two days now we should come have ye look at it. Hard to find the time."

The doctor glanced at Claire when Gram said her name. A quick flick of the eyes, but they held the same expression as when he'd stared a few moments ago. A little curious. But mostly…intense.

His touch was slow and gentle as he unwrapped the bandage. The first sight of burned flesh gripped Claire's stomach, bringing up memories she had to fight down. She tore her gaze away and focused on the doctor instead. He was muscular for a physician with broad shoulders and strong forearms revealed by his rolled sleeves. The sun streaming through the window brought out the red hues in his auburn hair.

The features on his face were bold and masculine, everything proportioned perfectly as if sculpted by an artist. No wonder Gram liked the man. Of course, Gram hadn't been able to see him for at least a year now. Could she possibly like him based on his personality? Not likely.

Doc Bryan frowned as he peered at Gram's injury, vertical lines gathering across the brow that had been smooth moments before. "It still hurts a good bit, doesn't it?" His voice became gentle and had that lilting quality she'd heard the first time he'd addressed Gram right after her injury.

"I can bear it." Gram's mouth pinched so much it almost disappeared.

Bryan glanced up at Claire again, and this time his gaze lingered. Searching her face as if looking for something. "It's not healing as well as I'd like. Could be her age. Could be the effects of the disease that caused her eyesight loss."

Claire nibbled her lip. That's what she'd thought, but hearing it spoken... "What can you do?"

He focused again on the hand. "Keep putting the salve on it twice a day. I'll send an herbal to help fight infection. Bring her back in three to four days, or if you see the redness spread or the blisters burst."

Swallowing, Claire nodded. With the extent of Gram's injury, a simple salve seemed so inadequate. Was that really all they could do?

Bryan closed the ledger where they kept their case notes and slid it back on the desk. The memory of Claire Sullivan's face when he'd discussed her grandmother's care played over and over in his mind. Was he doing enough to fight infection? The garlic tincture would help, as would the black walnut salve and the saleratus he'd mixed in. They needed to keep the blisters from bursting and give it time to heal. For some reason, Mrs. Malmgren's body had been slow to recover from all of her wounds these last few months. Was it just old age? Or something else he hadn't discovered? Maybe he should tell Alex to give her a full examination next time she came in.

Alex. Bryan lurched to his feet. He'd promised to head straight over to Alex and Miriam's house as soon as the last patient left. His brother had cornered him this morning and almost demanded Bryan come for dinner that night.

Good thing it was only a short walk to the little house next door to the clinic. Bryan breathed in the cooling air outside as he made the trek. The sun was just starting to set behind the mountains to the west. Normally, the fiery colors of a Montana sunset infused him with inspiration and hope. But he couldn't summon those emotions tonight.

Tomorrow he'd start his rounds in the mines again. So many of the miners suffered from chronic illnesses—most of them lung and breathing conditions. They couldn't leave work to attend the clinic, but at least he could go to them.

Ascending the two stairs to the stoop in front of Alex's house, Bryan tapped an alert on the wooden door, then nudged it open. "Anyone home?"

"Bryan, come in." Miriam looked up from pouring coffee at the little dining table.

Alex sat in his chair beside her, several papers in hand. "It's about time. I'd just about decided to come and send the patients away so you could eat."

A tickle of remorse climbed in Bryan's chest. "Sorry. Got caught up in paperwork."

One side of Alex's mouth pulled. "The log book that interesting, huh?"

Bryan fought the burn creeping up his neck. Time to move the conversation away from him. "Smells good, Miri." He slid into his usual chair around the four-person table.

Miriam lowered herself across from him and glanced sideways at her husband as she bowed her head.

"Father." Alex's voice filled the room. "Thank You for the food, and especially for the people at this table. I pray You'll give us strength and wisdom as we share Your love with those around us."

Bryan couldn't help but examine the way his brother spoke to the Lord. Earnestly. With reverence, sure, but as though he really believed God would give them strength and wisdom. Just because he asked.

At Alex's "amen," they loaded plates, and Bryan waited for the usual question to issue from his kid brother's mouth.

Alex filled his plate with shepherd's pie, then glanced at Bryan as he waited for the boiled apples to be passed around. "Who all came into the clinic today?"

Less than thirty seconds for the question to come. That had to be a record. If Alex couldn't stand to be away from his patients for one day a week, he should give up his day off.

Bryan took his time answering. He sent Miriam a polite smile when she handed the apples to him. After scooping a healthy portion on his own plate, he set the apples in front of Alex, careful to avoid the annoyed gaze shooting darts from Alex's eyes. Bryan bit back a smile. His younger brother was too feisty for his own good.

"Bryan." It was practically a growl.

He glanced up. "Yes?"

"Stop it."

The grin wouldn't stay. Bryan smirked at his brother, took one more bite of shepherd's pie, then leaned back in his chair. "It was a quiet day. Mrs. O'Leary came in for a check this morning. The baby seems to be growing nicely, not undersized like the last two."

Alex nodded. "Must be a girl then. Of her four, only the boys came out little."

"A new fellow came in with an abscessed tooth, a lackey from the smelter came in with a bad burn. Speaking of burns, Mrs. Malmgren's granddaughter brought her in for a check on that hand. Healing's slow, so I changed the salve and told her to rewrap it twice a day now." He'd worked hard to hold his voice steady for that last part.

A frown took over Alex's face. "Mrs. Malmgren's granddaughter is here? I hadn't heard."

"That's great," Miriam piped up. "I'll have to stop by and introduce myself."

Bryan tried to keep a sour look off his face. "You'll have to go to the café. Seems she's already taken a job there, although I thought her purpose in coming was to take care of her grandmother."

Miriam's forehead scrunched. "Aunt Pearl's?"

"Yep." At least she'd decided to serve meals there instead of the dozen or so saloons that also sold food. That was the only good thing he could say about the lady. Other than her gorgeous dark eyes that sparkled when she tried to hold in her anger.

His mouth pulled as another thought struck him. Was she such a hothead with everyone? Or was it only him that brought it out?

Claire forced the trip to the clinic from her mind as she loaded steaming plates onto her serving tray in the large café kitchen. Lilly stood at the work table with her back to Claire, slicing vegetables for the goulash. Dahlia, her one-year-old daughter, munched the cooked goulash in a chair. Neither spoke, which seemed to be the way of things in this kitchen. But something about the way Lilly wouldn't make eye contact suggested pain. Not rudeness like it had seemed that first day.

Raising the loaded tray to her shoulder, Claire turned and dipped her head to catch the child's eye. "Is that good, Dahlia?"

The little girl didn't speak, just bobbed her head once and stared down at her lap. Was the child that shy? Or did she take her cues from her mother? What was their story? Heartbreaking, most likely, if their skittishness were a side effect. Of course, maybe that was normal upbringing where Lilly grew up. Claire had pulled enough from the woman to know she was born in Guatemala from an English father and a native mother. No wonder she was so beautiful, with long black hair and refined features. But if Guatemalans were as prejudice as Americans tended to be, it wasn't hard to imagine how growing up in that household could be challenging.

With a last smile at Dahlia's bowed head, Claire shuffled toward the curtained doorway, straining to listen for footsteps amidst the hum of voices. Aha. She stepped aside as the fabric jerked and Aunt Pearl barreled through. Claire nibbled her lip against a smile. It'd taken three near-collisions for her to learn to stop and listen before venturing through that curtain.

While she delivered the plates of savory stew, Claire smiled and joked with the patrons. As much as she enjoyed spending time with Gram, meeting all these people and filling an obvious need for Aunt Pearl flooded Claire's veins with a rich satisfaction. These folks needed her and appreciated her help. What better feeling than that?

A man standing by the door caught her eye. He had to be a miner, considering that layer of black dust covering his rolled sleeves and suspenders, not to mention his face and arms. He had what Papa would have called an honest face.

"If you'd like to take a seat, sir, I'll pour your coffee and bring a plate. Special's goulash and corn bread, with cherry tarts for a sweet."

He twisted the cap in his hand, shuffling from one foot to the other and gnawing his lip. Poor man.

"Is there something I can help you with, sir?" Claire lowered the empty tray so it dangled from her right hand. The left arm ached from bearing the brunt of the load all evening.

"I, um… I need some food, four plates full. It's, um… My missus' birthday. It's hard on her now, so thought this'd be nice." His face flamed underneath the black dust, almost as bright as his chestnut hair.

A smile pulled at Claire's cheeks. "So you'd like us to package it? No problem. Have a seat, and I'll pour a mug of coffee while you wait."

He glanced around, ducking his head like a giant in a room too small. He must not make it out to eat very often. The man eased stiffly into the chair closest to the door.

Claire flipped the empty mug over and filled it from a coffee pot on a nearby table. "I'll be back in a few short minutes."

Back in the kitchen, Claire filled four jars with the goulash as Aunt Pearl bustled in.

"What's O'Leary doin' at the front table? Can't say as I've ever seen him in here, what with that brood he has to feed off'n only a miner's wage."

Claire spared a glance at the woman while her hands kept working. "Is he the man sitting by the door with the red hair? He's picking up food so his wife doesn't have to cook on her birthday. Isn't that sweet?"

A hazy look filtered over Aunt Pearl's gaze as she spooned stew onto plates. It could have been from the heat of the stove, but the catch in her voice raised a question. "It's sweet, all right. What with her expectin' and four kids pullin' her every direction."

Four kids and one more on the way? She did deserve a night off. Claire's mind played back to the little family she'd seen out Gram's window her first night in town. That mother had been within a month or two away from full-term. How many more women and children were scattered through this town full of rough men?

Which reminded her... Claire glanced at Aunt Pearl's back where she'd sunk her hands into wash water. "Aunt Pearl, is there another place in town where I could buy supplies for Gram? It seems what Mr. Lanyard's charging is a half-pence shy of thievery."

A chuckle drifted from the older woman. "I reckon' he does seem 'spensive compared to pricin' back East. And Bill Lanyard's personality's about as charmin' as a hungry bull." She turned from the bucket and dried her hands on a cloth. "He's got decent prices, though. And quality stuff. You could try the mercantile for some things, but they're more likely to be higher. For milk an' eggs an' meat, you could try to find a farmer outta town that'll sell to ya direct. That's not easy, though. And 'twouldn't be much cheaper than Lanyard. Believe me, I checked." Aunt Pearl's brows drew down in a rueful grimace. "If ye can get past his temperament, he's got the best place to shop."

"Oh. Thanks." Claire pinched her lips as she ducked her head and wrapped a half dozen cherry tarts in a cloth. It was hard to believe the prices she'd been quoted were the best in town, but Aunt Pearl would know.

So she might have to keep dealing with Mr. Lanyard, but as soon as she could pay off Gram's debt, she'd deal with the man on her terms.

Chapter Five

"Whoa, boy." Bryan eased back in the saddle and reined his gelding to a stop in front of the livery door. It'd been a long two days making rounds through the mountains. Some of the people needed a doctor but were too stubborn to come into town for it. Or maybe too short-handed to leave their ranches.

He scrubbed a hand through his hair, then slid from Cloud's back. It'd been nice to stay the night with Gideon and Leah Bryant, though. That new baby girl of theirs was a cutie. Just a month old and happy as a kangaroo in a pouch.

Bryan slipped the reins over the gelding's head and strolled inside the livery. "Jackson?"

A nicker sounded from deeper in the barn. Bryan slowed so his eyes could adjust to the dimness. "Anyone here?"

A ragged groan emanated from the recesses of the building. Bryan's senses came alive, nerves tingling down his spine. "Jackson, where are you?" He tossed the reins over a rail, then jogged down the long aisle. "Jackson?"

Another groan. Closer. Bryan slowed, the darkness thick in the stalls on either side. He veered to the left into the last doorway. It sounded like the moans had come from here.

The crumpled body of a man lay in the corner, surrounded by long splintery pieces. Bryan eased to his knees in front of the man. Was it a heart condition? "Where does it hurt?"

"Shoulder." Jackson said the word with a groan as he clutched his left arm.

Bryan reached out and touched the man's left elbow, then slowly ran his cupped hand up the arm. "Is it numb?"

"Nah." Jackson sucked a breath. "Burns like a knife in me."

When he touched the shoulder area, Jackson cried out. But Bryan kept his hand in place long enough to feel the soft spot where the humerus bone should have been, under the layer of shirt and skin. Definitely dislocated, but that was easier to heal than a heart condition.

Crouching back on his heels, Bryan inspected the man. "I need better light. Think you can walk to the front of the barn?"

Jackson grunted and held out his good hand. As Bryan pulled him to his feet, he peered at the chunks of wood scattered around him. His gaze traveled upward. Several more wooden pieces dangled from a jagged hole in the ceiling. Had he fallen through the loft?

Once on his feet, Jackson moved with stiff deliberation down the barn aisle toward the shining light filtering through the barn doors. Cloud nudged Bryan when they passed. "Wait a minute, boy." The horse heaved a sigh, then stood quietly.

Just inside the open front doors, Jackson turned to face Bryan, as if squaring off. "Fix me, Doc." His voice was hoarse. The pain must be eating him inside.

"Okay, let's lay you on the floor here." Bryan motioned toward some loose hay to the side where he'd have room to work.

With his jaw clenched and clutching his arm, Jackson dropped to his knees and allowed Bryan to help him ease back to the ground.

Bryan glanced around for something the man could hang onto. A rope on a hook was the only thing handy. Grabbing it, he pried Jackson's good hand from its strangle-hold on the wrist of the injured arm and slipped the braided leather into the man's grip. "Hold onto this."

Positioning himself on one knee, Bryan braced a foot against Jackson's left side. "I'm going to ease your arm toward me." He kept his voice low and strong as he slowly followed his own direction.

Jackson moaned through gritted teeth as Bryan steadily pulled the arm down and out.

"Oh." The man's grunt was followed by a sigh of relief, and his muscles relaxed in Bryan's grip. That must have done it.

"Feel better?" Bryan leaned forward to watch Jackson's face.

Jackson turned to him with exhausted gratitude shining in his eyes. "Much. Haven't hurt that bad since I broke my wrist. Maybe not even then."

The man struggled to sit up, and Bryan leaned forward to help. "Sit here for a minute and let me get something to wrap your arm."

A shuffling noise sounded from behind, and Bryan glanced back. Had Cloud left his ground-tied position?

Claire Sullivan stood in the doorway, sending his pulse into a leap stronger than the surprise warranted.

Bryan rose and faced her. "Miss Sullivan." What was she doing here? Surely she didn't need to rent a horse.

With the sun at her back, he couldn't see her expression. But her features tipped toward Jackson, and she took a tentative step in that direction. "I… I heard a moan. Is he hurt?"

"I took care of it." Did that harsh bark come from him? The way she shrank back made him want to lunge forward and take away the words. Why did he always lose his manners in front of this woman?

Then her shoulders squared, her china-doll chin rose, and she swept around him to kneel beside Jackson. The scent of honey wafted in her wake. "Where does it hurt, sir? Your wrist?"

Jackson's dirt-smeared face lit like Christmas morning. "My shoulder, ma'am. Doc put it in place, but I think it might help to wrap it up."

Bryan rolled his eyes and folded his arms across his chest, but no one was looking at him to see it. After all he'd done, this woman had only to waltz into the livery for Jackson to go silly. Just like when he was with Alex, Bryan had no choice but to fade into the shadows. But he couldn't force himself to turn away from the sight.

"I believe you're right." Claire reached up to stroke the man's shoulder.

Jackson's face turned red as chili peppers, and he glanced down at his fingers scrunching the hem of his shirt. "Aw, I'll be all right."

"I'm sure you will, Mr.…. What's your name, sir?"

"Jackson. Abraham Jackson, ma'am." His attention jerked to her face, then skittered away. Her beauty could have that effect. It was almost too much to take in without staring.

"Well, Mr. Jackson, I'm glad you're feeling better, but it would help your arm if we supported it for a few days." She spun to face Bryan. "Do you have a bandage in your pack we could use to make a sling?"

Now she needed him. "I do." But without uncrossing his arms or making any move toward his horse, he stood patiently in the barn aisle.

Her perfectly shaped brows gathered. "Where is it?"

Chagrin tugged at Bryan's chest. He shouldn't let this woman get in the way of his care for those who needed him. With a sigh loud enough to let her know she was imposing, he turned toward Cloud.

Once he had the bandage and sling in hand, he made his way back to where Miss Sullivan knelt beside Jackson, fussing over him. Bryan dropped to his knees behind the man. "We'll wrap your arm close to your body first, then support it with a sling. Keep this on two or three days, at least. All right?" He leaned around to glimpse the look on the livery owner's face.

A scowl, of course. "I guess, if it'll keep it from poppin' outta place again." The agreement probably wouldn't have been so reluctant if Miss Sullivan had done the asking.

While Bryan wrapped the arm and strapped it up, Jackson ate up every bit of Miss Sullivan's purring and coddling. She did have a kindness about her, and she'd obviously raised the man's spirits. But why couldn't she back off and let Bryan attend to business. *His* business. The work he'd been trained for at one of the most respected medical schools in the Northeast.

"There, Mr. Jackson. You keep this wrap on like the doctor said, and I bet it won't hurt again."

Jackson just grinned a goofy, bug-eyed smile.

Miss Sullivan leaned back and started to rise, and Bryan reached to assist. He may not like the woman, but it was time to dust off his manners.

"What's this?" She reached past his proffered hand and touched his shirtsleeve above the elbow. "You're hurt?"

When her fingers made contact with his skin without the fabric dividing them, a quiver ran through his arm. Pain mixed with…anticipation? *Get control of yourself, man.*

Bryan twisted to see the back of his triceps muscle. A bright circle of blood stained his shirt, outlining a tear about the size of his littlest finger.

Miss Sullivan stretched the ragged edges of the fabric apart. Her little intake of breath drew his eyes to her lips.

"It's deep. Looks like maybe from a nail or something rusty."

He jerked his attention away from her face and twisted his arm again to examine it. The gash was an inch long. No wonder it smarted. It looked deeper than a surface cut, but not enough to need a stitch. The brownish flecks around the edge of the wound did, indeed, look like remnants from something rusty.

"I just need to douse it with carbolic acid." He pulled away and strode toward Cloud and his saddle pack. His supply was low, but there should be enough for this little cut.

After pulling out a clean rag and the glass bottle, he turned and almost slammed into Miss Sullivan. "Pardon—"

"Oh—"

He gripped her arm with his free hand to keep her upright. That sweet honey scent tickled his senses again. "Sorry about that." His gaze wandered down to her face, and his hold on her arm tensed, drawing her closer.

For a split second she held his gaze, her mouth tipping as her teeth found her lower lip. Those lips.

His mouth went dry.

But he couldn't focus on them, because she turned away, pulling back from his hold. "Let me see your arm."

Bryan extended it, although why he obeyed he couldn't have said. But she didn't reach for the wounded area, instead touched the cuff at his wrist, her nimble fingers slipping the button loose. His breath came harder as she folded the fabric back, again and again. Working her way up to his elbow. Every time her fingers brushed his skin, goose bumps crawled up his arm. Over and over. No matter how he tried to look away, he couldn't break his stare. He swallowed, forcing himself to breathe.

She stopped one fold past his elbow, her gaze flicking to his before she bent over and peered at the injury. If only she'd look at his face with as much interest as she eyed the bloody cut on his arm.

"May I have the acid?"

He stared at her extended hand before his brain kicked in. "Oh, yeah." After he placed the bottle and cloth in her hand, his eyes tracked her every movement. Why was he so mesmerized?

She held up the vial and poured a tiny amount into his cut, bracing the cloth underneath to catch the liquid.

Sweet flapjacks and syrup. A sharp sting lit up his arm, jolting all his senses to vivid life, tearing him from any lingering remnants of his trance. Bryan sucked in a breath to keep from jerking his arm away or saying something he'd regret.

Chapter Six

Claire's hands still shook as she scurried down an alley toward Ottawa Street and Gram's house. What was it about that doctor that unnerved her so?

The heat of his gaze had burned up her neck as he'd watched her roll up his sleeve. It had made sense for her to do it, since she had two good hands to ease the fabric over his cut. She'd done it with other patients when she'd helped Papa. But with this man, the action had seemed so...intimate. Claire allowed a long breath to leak out. *Lord, help me keep my distance from him.*

As she approached the intersection, Claire's spirit weighed heavy. That wasn't the kind of request she should pray. He was one of God's creations, loved and formed in God's image. Pressing her eyes shut, Claire wrapped her arms across her chest and focused on that quiet place in her soul. *I'm sorry, Lord. Show me if there's something You want me to help him with.*

She paused, and moments later, the peace she'd been looking for crept into her soul. A calm pleasure sweeping over her. A rightness. *Thank you, Father.*

Opening her eyes, Claire resumed her journey back to Gram's house, just three doors down now. Maybe she'd have time to write a letter to Mama and Papa before heading back to the café to serve dinner.

A wagon stood on the edge of the street near Gram's house, its two mules dozing in the sunshine. Curious that the owner hadn't parked in front of the home or business they were visiting. Unless…

Claire gripped her skirts and strode faster to Gram's front door. As she paused for a second on the porch to compose herself, the sound of a man's laugh drifted through the wooden door. Not a deep baritone like Doc Bryan's. But definitely male.

She grabbed the handle and pushed it open. Sitting in the two upholstered chairs by the dormant fireplace were Gram and an older man Claire had never seen before. His gray hair formed an indentation of a hat brim, and his face wore the color and lines of many years under the sun.

"Clara Lee?"

"Hi, Gram." Claire strode to her grandmother's side and took up the outstretched hand in both her own. She eyed the stranger. "Hello."

The man rose. With the way his shoulders stooped, he stood at Claire's eye-level. "Howdy, Miz Sullivan. Yer Gram was jest tellin' me how tickled she is yer here." He stepped forward and gripped Claire's hand with a strong clasp.

"Hello." She'd already said that, but her mind struggled to muddle through all her questions. Who was this man? How did he know Gram so well? How much had they talked about Claire, that he knew not only her last name, but also the pet name she called her grandmother?

"Clara Lee, I'd like you to meet my dear friend Moses Calhoun." Gram waved her good hand in an elegant sweep toward the man. "He's just returned to town and stopped by to catch up."

"And how is it you know my grandmother, Mr. Calhoun?"

The man chuckled. Almost a cackle really. But the way his face folded into a toothy grin was contagious. It was hard not to smile, no matter how much she wanted to distrust the presence of a strange man in Gram's home.

"Well now. The doc's wife introduced us. Awful glad she did, too. Can't say I've ever met a gal quite as special as yer Gram."

The...doc's...wife. The words resounded in her mind, ricocheting there so the rest of the man's speech couldn't infiltrate her thoughts. The doctor was married? But of course he was. Why should it surprise her? The man was handsome—gorgeous really—with that auburn hair and a roguish hint to his expression that both challenged and drew everyone around him.

What was his wife like? A blonde beauty? Maybe a feisty red-haired Irish lass with vibrant blue eyes. Someone who could put up with his stubbornness, and maybe even give it back to him. Why did the thought of Bryan with a wife leave a sinking feeling in her chest?

"Feel how soft, Clara Lee."

Claire forced herself back to the present. Gram held up a folded piece of blue damask silk, a smile lighting her worn face so it shone. Claire's own heart lifted.

She reached to finger the material. Much softer than she'd expected. "It's lovely, Gram. Truly."

"It came all the way from Japan. Across the Pacific Ocean and over the mountains. Wasn't it special of Mose to bring it?"

Claire glanced up at the man, who stared at Gram as if every word she said were better than water in the desert. "Yes, it was very kind, Mr. Calhoun. However did you come by it?" And what in the Book of Genesis was going on between the two of them? Some kind of adolescent courting ritual?

"Please, Miz Sullivan. Call me Mose. Everyone does." He darted a glance at Gram. "Or Ol' Mose. That's the way most people say it." A flush crept into his cheeks.

"All right."

Gram's hand slipped into Claire's, squeezing gently. Claire ran a thumb over the wrinkled surface of Gram's skin and squeezed back. This man was special to her grandmother. The least she could do was get to know him.

Ol' Mose shuffled his feet. "Well, much as I'd rather stay an' keep company with the two prettiest ladies I'se ever seen, Zeb an' Zeke've been awful patient after this long trip. I'd best get'm settled in."

Gram released Claire's hand and pushed to her feet, then reached out to the man.

He took her hand in his and slipped her fingers through his elbow as though they were a young couple out for a moonlit stroll. "Miz Claire, I'm awful glad you're here. An' I'm especially glad you was here to help Miz Alice when that stove tried to fight back." He tossed a wink over his shoulder at Claire.

Claire tried her best to keep the amusement from her face. "I'm glad I was, too."

When the pair reached the door, Claire tried not to be conspicuous while she watched them.

Ol' Mose turned to face Gram and pressed a kiss to her good hand. "I'm hopin' you'll let me to pick ya both up fer dinner at Aunt Pearl's. You'd sure be the best comp'ny I've had since I was here last, an' I can't wait ta taste them blueberry pies you made."

A jolt ran through Claire. Aunt Pearl. Scurrying toward the sleeping chamber, she grabbed a fresh apron and glanced at herself in the mirror above the wash basin. One more pin would help contain her hair for the long evening ahead.

That done, she strode from the bedroom to find Ol' Mose and Gram still standing by the door. The man took a quick step away from Gram. Had he been whispering in her ear? Or something more? He held Gram's hand in his as he shuffled from one foot to the other.

A smile pushed its way onto Claire's face. She should probably be worried, but the two were so cute. "I have to get to the café. Will I see you both there for dinner?" Claire strode toward them and touched Gram's shoulder.

"Yes, dear. Moses is going to come back after he's taken the mules to the livery. We'll walk over together."

Claire glanced out the open door at the animals. "Sir, you may want to help Mr. Jackson. He took a fall today and needs to rest his shoulder."

Mose stepped onto the porch, settling his hat on his head. "I'll do it. Usually take care o' Zeb an' Zeke myself anyways." His mouth twitched as he gave her a sideways glance. "They tend ta get orn'ry if things ain't done jest so."

That toothy grin of his was hard to resist.

"Good. I'll head on now."

Claire lengthened her stride as she followed the path between Gram's house and the café. It was a blessing she'd delivered the blueberry pies earlier, as soon as the last ones came out of the oven. And good thing she'd made that last delivery for Aunt Pearl, or she wouldn't have come upon Doc Bryan and Mr. Jackson at the livery. Wouldn't have been there to tend the doctor's wound. She swallowed down the butterflies attempting to take flight in her midsection. Would he come into the café for dinner tonight? Did she want him to? And what about his wife? Would she accompany him?

Customers in the café were unusually scarce that evening. Maybe partially due to its being a Tuesday. By the time Gram and Mose came in, she'd served meals to the patrons and was refilling coffee cups.

"I've saved a quiet table here by the window for you." She motioned toward the corner, and Mose escorted Gram to where she pointed. Claire followed them over to help Gram settle into the chair, but Mose was already on the job. Easing her down, sliding her chair in. Interesting that Gram allowed him to do all that coddling. Definitely something going on between them.

After Gram was settled to his satisfaction, Mose moved around to his chair across the table and perched on the edge, taking Gram's good hand in his. It looked very much like the two had slipped into their own little world.

"I'll go get your food." Just in case they weren't too love-struck to eat. Claire spun and headed to the kitchen.

Aunt Pearl and Lilly worked-side by-side at the stove. Claire stopped at the counter beside them and loaded two plates of pork and cabbage onto her tray. "Do either of you ladies know a man named Moses Calhoun?" She tried to make the question sound casual.

Pearl tilted her head. "Calhoun. Oh, you mean Ol' Mose?"

"Yes, he said some people called him that."

The older woman chuckled. "Honey, everybody calls him that. Your grandma's the only one he lets call him Moses to his face. Didn't even know he had a last name until I heard her mention it." Aunt Pearl's gaze grew distant, her thin lips softening in a smile. "They sure are a sweet couple. Both of 'em with hearts o' gold. It's about time for him ta be back in town, I think."

Claire nodded toward the dining area. "He's out there now, treating Gram to dinner. For some reason, I didn't know about him." She raised her brows at Aunt Pearl. "Seems like a nice man, but I had no idea he was so important to Gram."

Aunt Pearl only shrugged. "'Tweren't my news ta tell. Far as I've seen, they've both been smitten since the day Doc Alex's wife introduced the two of 'em."

The words took several seconds to sink in. Doc Alex's wife? She felt like smacking her forehead. What a simpleton she was. How had she forgotten Bryan had a brother who also worked here as a doctor? And Gram had even told her that first morning how glad she was he'd married a sweet mountain girl. Hoisting the tray onto her shoulder, Claire spun and pushed through the curtain to hide her burning cheeks. Surely people would assume the flush was from the heat of the kitchen.

As she approached the table where she'd left Gram and Ol' Mose, Claire blinked to clear her vision. Another man had pulled up a chair. His tall back and broad shoulders were all she could see as he sat at the short end of the table facing away from her. But that familiar profile sent her chest into a heavy thumping.

Bryan? He wore a dark blue shirt now, not the white cotton with the torn sleeve he'd had on earlier.

As she approached the table, he turned and settled those greenish-brown eyes on her. The butterflies flitted in her stomach again. No need to be nervous around him. He was just a man. Same as Ol' Mose or Papa or her older brother Marcus. Of course, this man didn't have decent manners like the others. Couldn't keep a civil tongue in his mouth.

The doctor's chair scraped as he slid it back and stood with a respectful nod. That was a little mannerly. Ol' Mose followed suit, and she motioned them both down again.

"I only brought two plates, but I'll go get another." She kept her gaze focused on the tables so she didn't make eye contact with him.

"I'd appreciate it."

The richness in his voice pulled her attention despite her best efforts. Claire's gaze took in the roguish tilt of his mouth, the way one brow raised a little higher than the other. The strong curve of his cheekbones. She swallowed and spun away. "I'll be back."

She couldn't have said whether she spoke to Pearl or Lilly in the kitchen, but as she approached the table in the front corner again, her ears strained for any words in their conversation. Ol' Mose was telling a story with animated expressions, his hands spreading to add emphasis to his words. He was humorous to watch, with a demeanor that brought a smile no matter what her mood. Too bad Gram couldn't see him.

Claire's eyes flickered to her grandmother. Gram's milky gaze stared ahead, a smile tickling her mouth as she listened to every nuance of Mose's voice. Sight or not, she enjoyed this man. That much was obvious. A warmth washed through Claire, but a pang quickly replaced it.

She'd always clung to her only memory of Grandpop, from that time they visited North Carolina when she was five. Gram and Grandpop had so many wonderful years. Gram's letters had always shared news and messages from him. Now that it'd been over a year since his death, was it that easy for her to move on? Claire counted back the months in her mind. Almost two years really. Gram must be lonely in the house by herself. And how much easier would it be for her with another person around?

But this man was a freighter. A man who drove his wagon across the Montana Territory for a living. How could Gram ever have a life with him? Did Gram even want that?

Maybe she was jumping to conclusions. Maybe Ol' Mose was just a friend who Gram liked to visit with when he came to town.

A laugh burst from the table. Gram gasped and clasped her hand to her mouth, but she couldn't contain another chortle. Bryan's deep baritone joined in, and Claire's feet carried her forward of their own accord.

She placed the plate in front of the doctor and eyed the three of them. "Something must be funny here."

Gram wiped tears from her eyes as she continued to chuckle. "Moses tells the best stories. I declare."

"Jest sharin' life experiences, darlin'."

Chapter Seven

"But is it safe for you to ride alone in the wagon with that man?" Claire placed a hat pin in Gram's hand and watched her feel along the brim of the straw bonnet and insert the long metal rod. "Where's he taking you?"

Gram might think it was harmless, but riding by herself with a strange man was *not* safe. Especially when she couldn't see where they were going.

Gram reached out, and Claire slipped her hand into Gram's. "Clara Lee, I trust Moses. He's a good man. Most of the people here have known him for years and would trust him with their lives. *I* trust him with my life." Was the hitch in her tone only the quiver of an aging voice? "You go to the café like you normally do. I'll be enjoying the beautiful sunshine and the pleasant company."

Running her free hand over her hair, Claire sighed. "All right. But I'm going to ask him where he's taking you."

A chuckle followed as the older woman gripped her cane and thumped from the sleeping chamber into the kitchen.

While Ol' Mose assisted Gram into the wagon, Claire extracted from the man every possible route he might take to each destination he planned. By the time he shuffled back around the front of the mules, she couldn't think of any other questions.

He stopped in front of her and slipped his hands over one of hers. "Miz Claire. You rest assured I'll take the best care o' yer Gram I ever could. She means more ta me than I'm willin' ta say jest yet. I'm awful glad she agreed ta spend her day with me, and you can bet I don't want t'either of ya worrin'."

Staring into the man's face, she could see he cared. The stark earnestness outlined in his eyes by the deep grooves couldn't be simulated. "All right. You two enjoy the pretty day."

When the wagon drove away, Claire stepped back inside the house. What now? She'd dusted and swept and scrubbed the place again this morning, so there wasn't much else to do in the little cottage. They'd already baked the bread for lunch at the café, and there wasn't enough time to bake the pies for after dinner. Maybe Aunt Pearl would be okay with her coming early to the café. Lilly worked so hard to prepare the meal. Surely she'd appreciate an extra set of hands.

Gathering the two overloaded crates of bread, Claire traipsed to the back door of the café and let herself in. Lilly glanced up from her seat by the work table, and a hint of a smile touched her face when their eyes connected. That was progress. Even the glance was more than the woman usually gave.

"I hope it's okay that I'm early. Gram went out with a friend, so I thought I could help." Claire heaved the boxes onto the counter by the stove and brushed her hands as she turned to scan the room. "Where's the little one?"

Lilly paused from slicing ham and pointed the carving knife toward a pallet of blankets in the corner.

Claire searched the quilts in the dim area. At last her gaze found the sweet little face, eyes closed and fist balled near her mouth. So serene. "She's beautiful, Lilly. When does she turn two?"

"August twenty-second." The woman's speech was so perfect, her enunciation distinct, but with just enough lilt to sound forced. Like she was trying to be something she wasn't.

"I know you're proud."

Lilly ducked her head to focus on the meat as she sliced. Claire pulled a loaf from the top crate and settled in the empty chair beside Lilly to slice it.

For a while, they worked in companionable silence. What could she ask that wouldn't sound like prying and wouldn't make the woman uncomfortable? Claire pursed her lips. There was such a mystery about these two. A tragedy just under the surface. A need she wanted so much to fill.

"How long have you worked here with Aunt Pearl?" That should be innocuous enough.

"Two and a half years."

"My. That's quite a while. Did you live in Butte before that, or had you just come?"

"A couple months before." Lilly's hand sawed faster at the meat.

A nervous reaction from being questioned? Or anger as she remembered a story from the past? Either way, Claire should stop pressing for details Lilly obviously didn't want to share.

After Claire had sliced all the bread in her first box, a movement from the corner caught her attention. Dahlia reached forward in a cat-like stretch, then sat up, her fine dark hair rumpled on one side. Adorable.

Claire set down her knife and circuited the table to crouch in front of the little girl. "Hi, Dahlia. Did you get a good sleep?"

The little head bobbed, eyes wide until a yawn took over her face.

"Would you like to come have a slice of fresh bread and butter? I made the bread with my Gram."

The nod was slighter this time, and Dahlia ducked a little at the end, like she wasn't sure she should have said yes.

"Come over here, then." Claire held out her hand, and Dahlia's little fingers slid into it. Warmth started in Claire's palm where the precious little hand trusted hers, and the heat crept all the way up to her chest.

Claire sat at the table and settled Dahlia in her lap with a still-warm slice of bread spread with blackberry jam. The jam was a splurge, but Aunt Pearl doted on the child and surely wouldn't mind.

"Where is Aunt Pearl today?" Claire asked the other woman.

"She took food to the doctor's clinic for sick patients." Lilly brushed a lock of Dahlia's hair behind her ears before she resumed slicing the wedge of cheese in front of her.

Claire's attention jumped to alert at the mention of the doctor. "I suppose you've met the doctor several times, since you've lived here so long."

"Yes. Doctor Alex and his wife are very nice. Miriam is kind to my Dahlia."

Hmm… "I haven't met them yet, actually. Although I'd like to. I've only seen the other brother, Bryan."

A real smile actually bloomed on Lilly's face. "Doctor Bryan is an angel. A gift from God. He helped my Dahlia come into the world, and for that I'll always be grateful."

An angel? That had to be stretching it a bit. Still, Lilly seemed to have few people to rely on. Being grateful to the man who helped with the successful birthing of this little cherub was natural. Although the glow on Lilly's face at the mention of the doctor was a little much. Interesting.

A large hole in the ground loomed in front of Bryan. Cables rising from the bottom all the way to the massive pulleys dangling from the top of the headframe, about fifty feet in the air. All was quiet except a periodic rumble that sounded a bit like snoring.

With the pack over his shoulder, Bryan stepped through the open door at the base of the towering wooden structure.

A clatter sounded from the raised platform where the elevator operator worked.

"Halsten?" Bryan craned his neck to see up.

The noise of wood on wood, boot thuds, then a head of dark, bushy hair and beard peered over the edge. "Doc. Didn't 'spect ta see you today."

Bryan held in a grin. "Need to go down an' see a few men. Do you mind?"

"Naw." Halsten's head disappeared from the platform edge. "Jest give me a few minutes ta bring 'er up."

"Appreciate it."

Within a quarter hour, the top of the elevator cage appeared, rising up from the murky hole like a slow-moving geyser. Bryan slid between the wooden slats onto the swaying platform. "Ready."

The rickety contraption shook and creaked and swung about as it lowered. The ride up or down always seemed to take hours. It helped if he took his mind off the cage that carried him, and he had to force himself not to think about whether Halsten had inspected the cables recently. He shifted his stance to make up for the extra weight of the pack on his shoulder. The whole enclosure rattled and groaned with his activity. He stilled. No more movement until he reached the bottom of this pit.

Bryan inhaled a steadying breath. At least the extra heaviness in his bag was exciting. The masks Alex had commissioned from friends in Montreal finally arrived. They were a new design, made with a filter to cleanse the air of impurity as the person wearing the mask inhaled. The exhaled air was routed by a flange through a different opening, similar to the way a human's epiglottis allowed air through the windpipe but redirected food through the esophagus. An amazing design. *Lord, please help these masks work. Help the men be willing to wear the things.*

When he stepped off the elevator at the floor of the main shaft, Bryan greeted the miners he met by name. He'd worked hard over the last two years to build trust and rapport with the men. It helped that they didn't have to pay for his services, thanks to the generosity of Gideon and Leah Bryant, who paid his wages. Good people, the Bryants were. A special breed.

A loud, hacking cough sounded around a corner. Not an unusual sound in these dusty mines. Bryan followed the noise and spotted the first of the three men he'd come to see in the south shaft. O'Leary carried three sledge hammers over each shoulder, his back bowed under the load.

After jogging to catch up, Bryan settled into step beside the man. "How are you, Thomas?" He'd take part of the load if he could, but knew from experience the man wouldn't let him. Any sign of shirking could be cause for a worker's pay to be docked in mines. And with four kids at home and his wife expecting their fifth, Thomas O'Leary needed every penny he could scrounge.

Thomas bobbed a nod. "All right."

"I just received a shipment of something I'm pretty excited about." Bryan flipped open one side of his pack, and pulled out one of the contraptions. "It's a breathing mask. You wear it while you're working down here, and it filters the air you breathe, so you're not taking in all this dust that makes you sick."

O'Leary glanced sideways at the piece but didn't slow his trudging. Neither did he speak.

Bryan extended the apparatus toward him. "Would you like to try it? I think it'll help us get rid of that cough."

The man eyed the mask again, mouth pinched and brows raised. "Reckon' I can. Might as well."

A rush of relief surged through Bryan. "Great."

When they reached O'Leary's destination, Bryan helped fit the mask to his patient's face, then stepped back. "I'll come back to check on you in a day or two, see how it's going."

Thomas only nodded. It might take him a little while to get used to talking through the cover. But if the mask helped clear up the congestion in the man's lungs, it would likely save his life. And with so many miners dying of lung sickness, that would be a miracle, indeed.

Every visit to the upper level of these saloons made Bryan's chest ache and left him angry enough to pommel someone. He let himself out of one of the private rooms in The Irish Castle and trudged down the stairs.

The weary-faced woman he left had used her own methods to end a pregnancy, and nearly bled to death in the process. Finally he'd stopped the bleeding, and if she stuck to the diet he prescribed, her blood supply should rebuild itself. She'd be hard-pressed to *work* in the meantime, though. If only he could change her situation completely. And that of every one of these women.

At the base of the stairs, Bryan slipped through the wide door leading into the main saloon. The room was surprisingly empty, even for this time of morning.

And quiet. The loud clearing of a man's throat was the only sound in the stillness.

Bryan stopped and scanned the area, his eyes finding the bar.

Two men stood there. Chap, the giant of a bartender, had both hands raised in the air over his head. Another man, a stranger, stood on the front side of the counter. The rifle in his hand pointed at Chap, but his eyes could have glared a hole in Bryan.

"Drop your bag and raise your hands. You make any quick moves, and the barkeep's dead."

Chapter Eight

$\mathcal{B}$ryan obeyed the armed man's command, ignoring the sweat dripping down his back.

"Now get over next to him where I can see ya." The gunman bobbed his head toward Chap.

Bryan eased the twenty or so feet to the bar.

"That's far enough." The man focused again on Chap. "Now finish fillin' that sack."

Chap obliged, lowering his large frame to fill a leather bag with smaller satchels from a box under the counter. His movements were methodical, slow and measured.

Bryan took the opportunity to study their captor. The man was mid-sized and wore a neck scarf to cover the lower half of his face. A balding hairline revealed reddened skin on his forehead, like he'd spent too much time in the sun. He wore the shirt and vest of a gentleman, although the weave was a bit threadbare. The top button of his collared shirt opened to reveal dark chest hair. Nothing about the man looked familiar.

After a minute or so, with Chap working in steady motions, the robber shifted from one foot to the other, and his grip on the Winchester rifle tightened. "Move quicker," the man barked.

Over the course of another minute, beads of sweat ran down the gunman's forehead. His gaze flicked back and forth from Chap to Bryan, and occasionally, he glanced at the closed front door of the bar. He must have locked it when he cleared out the mid-morning patrons.

At last, Chap had the final small satchel stuffed in the large sack and rose to his feet.

"Hand it here," the man barked, reaching across the counter.

Chap obeyed. He was a large man, and his methodical movements came across as slow-witted at times. But Bryan knew from their conversation while he'd stitched the man after breaking up a barroom brawl, Chap had once studied under one of the finest lawyers in Boston. He'd hated the stress, though, and came west to see what adventure he could find. Surely, here at the wrong end of this stranger's gun, he'd found adventure enough.

Bryan focused on the man behind the rifle. His movements were jerky now, probably excited to be so near pulling off his heist. Would the man just leave with the money? *Lord, let it be.*

"Both of you. Get down on yer bellies." The Winchester gestured at the open floor in front of Bryan.

Shooting a glance at Chap, Bryan eased down onto his stomach.

"I'll have this rifle trained on ya 'til I ride outta sight, so don't even think about followin'. Get it?"

"Yessuh'." Chap's voice came out almost as a grunt.

Bryan tried to crane his neck to watch the man leave the building without raising his head. They were almost safe, and the last thing he wanted to do was rile the robber.

The thief backed toward the door, the oversized sack cradled in one hand like a precious child. With the other, he gripped the rifle, still trained on the two of them. At the closed front door he paused, seeming to struggle with how to remove the brace without losing his grasp on either precious possessions. He finally used the butt of the rifle to lift the metal bar from its holding arms. The rod clattered to the floor, and Bryan forced his muscles not to jump as the noise rang through the quiet saloon.

Outside sounds rushed in as the door opened and the thief backed out. He'd started to close the door when he heard the crash of wood. A loud groan, and the man crumbled to the sidewalk outside.

Bryan pushed himself up to his knees to get a better look. His muscles tensed, ready to spring up or flatten himself, depending on what he saw. The robber was, indeed, lying on the wooden boardwalk. The door creaked as a face peered around the edge.

Lurching to his feet, Bryan lunged forward. That face. It couldn't be.

The door opened wider, and Miss Sullivan's wide eyes scanned the room, then landed on him.

"What are you doing?" Bryan stopped himself in front of the woman just before he reached her, barely stopping himself from grabbing her shoulders and shaking them. "That man had a rifle and was nervous enough to point and shoot at anything that startled him. You almost got yourself killed." He sucked in deep breaths, trying to slow his racing pulse.

She blinked, then glanced down at the heap of unconscious man beside her, lying in the midst of splintered wood and some kind of gray, lumpy sauce.

Dropping to one knee, Bryan laid two fingers on the man's neck. His pulse was strong. Moving his fingers under the robber's nose, a steady flow of air tickled Bryan's skin. Breathing just fine. Bryan shifted to the man's eyes, raising both lids at the same time. The left pupil shrank against the bright sunlight. The right did as well, but only half as much. A concussion for sure, but the man would likely be coming around soon.

Glancing up, relief flooded Bryan at the sight of Chap hovering over them. "He'll wake soon with a headache, but he should be fine in a few days. Now's a good time to get him to the jail."

"It'd be my pleasure. Let me put this bag in a safe spot, an' I'll take care o' that weasel." Chap hoisted the sack of money and disappeared into the dark interior.

Bryan picked up the Winchester the man had dropped in his fall, then rose and turned his full attention to the woman who'd just shaved ten years off his life. "Don't ever approach a man who's pointing a loaded gun. Got it?"

The blood rushed through him again as he took in her pretty face. A face that could easily be lying dead on the ground right now if things had turned out differently.

Miss Sullivan raised those pretty brows. "You're welcome."

Air left his lungs in a whoosh. He dropped his gaze and scrubbed a hand through his hair. "I'm sorry. I..." She was right. He raised his eyes to meet hers. "Thank you."

Her face softened a little, and she glanced down at the man still unconscious on the ground. "Did he hurt you?"

"No. Seemed like he was only after the money." He scanned the viscous brown gunk splattered across the wooden sidewalk. "What did you hit him with?"

She nibbled her lower lip. "A crate full of Aunt Pearl's dumplings. I was out making deliveries, and I saw he had a gun pointed at someone inside, and I just...reacted." She peered up at him. "I'm glad you weren't hurt."

Chap reappeared in the doorway and, in a smooth motion, reached down, grabbed the robber, and swung him onto his broad shoulder. The limp form moaned, but Chap ignored it. Bryan handed over the rifle, and Chap took it with a nod. He turned toward Miss Sullivan, touched the rifle barrel to his forehead in salute, and said, "Much obliged, ma'am."

She dipped a quick curtsey. "Glad you're okay, and glad I could help."

"So he didn't get away with the money?"

Bryan kept his face stoic as he forked another beef chunk and dragged it through the gravy on his plate. "Didn't get away at all."

Miriam's eyes grew round as silver dollars. "How'd you stop him?"

The crowd around them at the café made it hard for his silence to have its full effect. "Miss Sullivan got the better of him and knocked him unconscious."

Alex's mouth twisted in a curious grin, but he stayed quiet. He didn't have to talk near as much now that he was married. Miriam's brow knit in confusion, then flew up as she leaned forward. "Mrs. Malmgren's granddaughter? What was she doing there? In a saloon and…a brothel?"

Hmm… He should probably clear up the reasons soon, but it was fun dragging out the suspense.

A motion at the corner of his eye caught his attention. There she was. An apron covering the same blue dress she'd worn earlier. Hair pulled back in a knot. Eyes…stunning.

Miss Sullivan strode right to their table, her left arm supporting a tray of steaming plates. He tried to catch her gaze, but she wouldn't look at him. As she placed a dish in front of each person, the table fell silent. Something struck his shin under the table, but he ignored it.

Miriam drummed her fingers on the table, then cleared her throat just as Miss Sullivan started to turn away. "Are you Mrs. Malmgren's granddaughter?"

She rotated back, her gaze darting to Bryan before it settled on Miriam. Now she looked at him? "Yes."

Miriam thrust out her hand. "I've been eager to make your acquaintance. Bryan's said so much about you, I feel like you're already a friend. I know your grandmother's thrilled to have you here." She sank back in her chair with a sappy smile at Alex. "She's a special favorite with us."

Bryan gripped his hands together under the table to keep from clamping one over the magpie's mouth. *Bryan's said so much about you?* When had he said *so much*?

But the damage was done. Miss Sullivan raised a brow at him, then turned back to face his mouthy sister-in-law. "It's a pleasure, Mrs. Donaghue. My grandmother speaks highly of you all."

"I've been meaning to pay a visit to check on you both, but things have been so busy at the clinic. Would it be okay if I do that?"

Miss Sullivan tipped her head the slightest bit as she studied Miriam, exposing her elegant neck as her hair brushed to the side. Bryan swallowed to bring moisture back to his mouth.

"I'd like that." She motioned around the dining room. "I help serve lunch and dinner, so morning or afternoon would be best."

A glimmer in Miriam's eye caught his attention away from the beauty standing beside him. "Perfect. That way you can tell me all the details about how you saved Bryan from the robber."

Bryan shot her a dark look, but Miriam ignored him.

A blush stole over the woman's pretty cheeks. "I was in the right place at the right time, I suppose."

Bryan clamped his jaw against a retort. This woman's good deeds were going to get her in trouble one day.

Claire stifled a yawn as she replaced the coffee pot on the stove the next morning. Images of the robber had plagued her dreams all night and stolen her energy this morning. Sometimes he held Bryan at gunpoint, while all she could do was stand there open-mouthed. Not even able to scream. In other images, she was the one with the cold, metal gun barrel pressed to her chest, while Bryan lay on the ground in a bloody mess.

She scrubbed a hand over her face. Only dreams.

Picking up both coffee mugs, she turned and shuffled toward the front door. Gram had risen earlier than normal this morning and already sat rocking on the front porch.

"The coffee smells good." Claire eased a cup into Gram's hands, careful to keep her hold until Gram took the weight of the mug.

"It does, Clara Lee."

When Claire had settled into her own rocker, Gram reached over, her hand patting the wooden arm until she found Claire's. Gram's mouth formed a soft smile. "Have I told you lately how glad I am you came?"

"I'm glad, too." And she was. Looking at her grandmother now, Claire's heart ached with love for the woman. For all the years they could have shared, if only the distance hadn't separated them.

"I have good friends here in Butte, but there's nothing quite as special as having family to share life with."

"I agree." Claire leaned against the chair and rocked, eyeing the orange rays rising over the distant mountain range. What were Mama and Papa doing at home this morning? Papa probably sat in his chair at the table, reading some medical publication while Mama scurried around the kitchen preparing breakfast.

"In fact, there's something I'd like to share now, and I'm glad you can be the first to know."

Claire turned to watch Gram's face. Why the hesitation in her voice? "What is it?"

A smile lit her features, the wrinkles forming an expression that made her look ten years younger. "Moses asked me to marry him."

She had to blink twice before the words would register. "Marry?"

A soft pressure squeezed Claire's hand. "Yes, honey. Marry."

"But why? When?" Why in the world would Gram think about marrying again? That would be too much for her. How dare this man ask it? Did he have no concept of what Gram was going through, trying to adjust to losing her sight?

"I told him yes."

"Gram, you can't mean that." Claire fought the urge to leap from the chair. How could Gram sit there and talk about this calmly? "How can you possibly… I mean, what…?" Ugh. How could she say this without insulting her grandmother?

"Clara Lee." Gram's voice softened. "I may be old and blind, but that doesn't mean I want to stop living. I loved your Grandpop. We were a good match, together a lot of years." There was a catch in Gram's throat, and she paused. Claire looked over for signs of distress, but Gram sat peacefully, a kind of wistful smile on her face.

At last, Gram took a deep breath. "He's gone to a better place, though. He sure wouldn't want me to sit here and pine for 'im." She squeezed Claire's hand again. "Moses makes me laugh like I haven't in years. That man is special, and he makes me happy."

Claire swallowed past the knot in her throat. "I'm glad, Gram. I want you to be happy. It's hard not to worry, though." She studied her grandmother. How lonely had she been since Grandpop died? It must have been hard, to live so many decades with a man, then suddenly be alone. Mose and Gram did seem to enjoy each other. "Is he going to retire, then, and stay in town?"

Gram's mouth pulled into a smile, one corner tipping higher than the other. "He offered that, but I told him I'd rather ride along with him. Might as well enjoy the countryside instead of sittin' here all day."

Claire sucked in a breath, but it caught somewhere in her airway, forcing coughs that bent her over. It was several moments before she could breathe a steady gulp.

"You gonna make it, dear?"

Nodding, Claire pressed a hand to her chest. "Oh, Gram." What had her grandmother gotten herself into?

As the silence settled over them, Claire sank into the rocking of her chair. What was she going to do now? Would Gram need her at all after the wedding? It didn't sound like it. So did that mean she should go home? What reason would there be to stay? Even if the idea of leaving formed a sick knot in her stomach.

Chapter Nine

Claire tightened her grip on the crate of food and forced her legs to move faster. According to Lilly's directions, that shanty up ahead had to be the one. Good thing, because her arms wouldn't have made it much farther with this load.

The sound of a child crying drifted through the cracks in the wood as Claire neared the door. She allowed the box to sink to the ground with a *thunk* and leaned on the sides of the box to catch her breath. Who would have thought a crate of food would be so heavy?

A second child started wailing inside the shack, his voice a little older than the first. Claire rose and inhaled a final deep breath, then raised her hand to knock on the worn wood of the door. A chunk was missing from the base, and as the crying grew louder inside, a gray skirt appeared in the opening below.

The door pulled open a crack, and the face of a weary woman peered down at her from the stoop. "What is it?"

Claire motioned to the crate on the ground beside her and spoke up over the crying child. "I brought food. I work at the diner with Lilly. I mean, Mrs...." What was Lilly's last name? Oh, well. "She said your children were sick, so I brought stew and fresh bread that were left from lunch." Stopping for a breath, she watched the woman eye her another second.

Finally, the mother stepped back and pushed the door open to reveal a child on her hip and a protruding midsection. The little red-haired lad stopped crying when he saw her, his splotchy face almost as red as his curls.

"'Preciate it." The woman motioned across the room. "You can set it on the table. I gotta get back to Malcom and the girls." She swept away, disappearing through the inner doorway that appeared to split the small home in two. The door closed behind her, muffling the whimpers and whines of the children.

Claire set to work, falling into the familiar routine she used whenever she visited sick families around Charlotte. Heat emanated from the cook stove, so she wouldn't have to go near the fire inside. *Thank you, Lord.* She'd been forced to feed the fire at Gram's these past few weeks, but she'd take any chance she could to avoid those painful memories.

She scrubbed out the big pot on the back of the stove top. It looked as if it hadn't seen a good cleaning for months, but the crusty layers of food were gone by the time she rinsed it off. She'd used most of the water from the bucket in the dry sink, so fetching clean water moved up on her list of things to do before she left this place. The fire was going nicely now, and as she dumped the stew from the jars into the clean pot, a tap sounded on the door. Mrs. O'Leary and the children hadn't come out of the back room. Should she answer it?

"O'Learys." That deep voice was unmistakable. "It's Doc Bryan."

A torrent of emotions flooded Claire as she stepped to the door. Her pulse quickened even while relief eased the tension in her muscles. Those poor children did need a doctor. And from what she'd seen with his care of Gram at the clinic, and again with Mr. Jackson at the livery, this man seemed to know what he was doing.

Claire lifted the latch and peeked out before swinging the door wide.

He stood on the stoop and blinked at her, then his face tipped into a tense smile. "Miss Sullivan. Didn't expect to see you here. Heard a rumor my friends weren't feelin' so good." He peered around her. "Mind if I come in and check on 'em?"

"Of course." She stepped aside and returned to the stove. The stew needed her attention before it scorched. Or at least she could act like it did. "Mrs. O'Leary's in the back room with the children. I brought some stew."

He stopped in the center of the room, and she could feel his gaze searing her back as she stirred the beef and vegetable mixture. Was he waiting for her to let Mrs. O'Leary know he'd come?

"Doc Bryan!" The child's voice pierced the air, and Claire jerked her head up in time to see a blur of red curls fly through the room.

The doctor swung the lad up in his arms, this one older than the child Mrs. O'Leary had held. "My buddy. How goes it, lad?" Bryan's rich voice slipped into an Irish brogue.

The boy's freckled nose scrunched. "I feel lousy, but Mama says the girls are worse off than me and Sid, an' I shouldn't complain."

Bryan chuckled. "Always do what Mama says." He lowered the lad to the floor with one arm, even though the boy had to be at least five or six. "Let's go see what we can do to help the girls."

Claire's heart ached to follow them as the pair disappeared into the back room. Who was that man with the easy smiles and affection for the child?

They left the door open, and Claire strained to decipher the murmurs drifting from the room. The soft voice of the woman, higher pitches of children, and the deep baritone of the doctor. She listened so hard, she would have sliced her finger open while cutting bread if the knife were any sharper. Claire narrowed her eyes at the dull blade. Maybe she could find a whetstone before she left.

The stew in the pot bubbled, and Claire shifted it to the back surface. She glanced at the open door. Would they want to eat now?

Stepping softly on the balls of her feet, she crept toward the door. "Mrs. O'Leary?" She hated to disturb them, especially while the doctor was here.

Doc Bryan's voice murmured something low, then the woman called. "Come in."

Claire's shoulders eased. As she leaned through the doorway, it took her a moment to adjust to the brighter light. A window of greased parchment on the long side of the room allowed in sun, which was more than the front living area could boast. Three beds lined the chamber. A rope tied across the ceiling, and a sheet hung from it. Right now, it was bunched at one end, separating the far bed from the first two.

Two figures lay in each of the near beds, and Doc Bryan bent over one, listening through a Camann's stethoscope to a girl with long, auburn hair. Another girl lay beside her in the bed, her face a younger version of the first. The sisters bore a striking resemblance to their mother, albeit with paler faces and without the worry lines.

Bryan rose and folded the medical apparatus. "Well, Cathleen, I think you're ready for some warm broth." He glanced up at Claire. "Maybe some of that good stew Miss Sullivan brought." His gaze found the other girl in the bed. "You can try it when you're ready, Miss Audrey."

Mrs. O'Leary stood beside the child and stroked the mussed hair from her forehead. "Thank you, Doctor. We'd be in a fix without you. Thomas said the breathing mask you gave him already cleared up his cough."

Bryan's attention jerked to her face. "Did he?" The hint of a smile touched his lips, but his eyes reflected the full grin he must be holding back. "I'm glad."

What kind of breathing mask? Claire scanned her mind. Papa hadn't ever prescribed such a device that she could remember.

"I'll spoon soup for the wee ones." Mrs. O'Leary stepped toward her, waking Claire from her thoughts.

She strode toward the kitchen area ahead of the woman. "I sliced bread for them, too. And brought jam from the café." When she turned to face the woman as she spoke, the bulge at her waistline caught Claire's attention. Mrs. O'Leary must be at least eight months pregnant.

Claire examined the woman's face closer. This was the woman who had passed by Gram's house that first night, when Doc Bryan doctored Gram's hand. A sudden kinship washed through her.

"Is there anything else I can do to help? I need to get back to Aunt Pearl's, but could spare another minute."

Moisture sparkled in the young mother's eyes as she scanned the food and other contents of the crate on the counter. "Not a thing."

Something compelled Claire forward to place a hand on the woman's shoulder. "You have a heavy load. I'll come back and check on you tomorrow morning."

Mrs. O'Leary dropped her gaze to her, her fingers fumbling with the edge of her apron. "You don't havta do that."

Bryan's voice from the other room drowned out Claire's opportunity to reply. "If ye lads allow yer Mum an hour's rest every day, I'll bring some next time I come. Do we have a deal?"

Both women turned to watch the doctor as he escaped the bedroom with a grin. Calls and choruses trailed him through the open door. "I'll need a full report, ma'am." Bryan turned the full force of the grin on Mrs. O'Leary. "So we can decide if they earn their toffee."

Something in Claire's chest yearned for that smile to turn toward her. A hint of boyishness, mixed with the strength of this man. Butterflies fluttered in her stomach.

"I'll do that," Mrs. O'Leary murmured.

Bryan's nod seemed to close the subject. And then he did turn his full focus on Claire. The butterflies multiplied.

"Miss Sullivan, I'm headed to Aunt Pearl's. Would you like an escort?"

"I, um…" She jerked her chin up. Maybe that would open the airway so her brain could start working. "Yes, thank you."

Spinning back to Mrs. O'Leary, she rested a hand on the nearest chair back. "I'll stop by tomorrow morning. Send for me at the café if there's anything else you need."

The other woman nodded. "I know where your grandmum lives, but we'll be fine. Much obliged to you both for the food and doctorin'."

Claire gathered the crate of empty jars and positioned it on her left hip. With a wave, she preceded the doctor from the little home. Outside, she breathed a deep gulp of fresh air as he fell into step beside her.

"The air gets kinda stale in a sick house, huh?" His words were a bit of a surprise. He didn't seem the type for small-talk.

She shot him a closed-mouth grimace. "Didn't realize it until I came out here."

Silence again. Should she break it? Do the polite thing Mama would expect and discuss the weather? She'd really like to ask about the breathing mask.

"It was nice of you to bring food for them." Bryan's voice held a casual tone. Not the brusque efficiency she'd grown used to.

"I heard they were sick, and there was leftover food, so…" She struggled to find a way to shed the credit. "It was nice of Aunt Pearl to send it." She wanted to turn and look at him, but that would be too much like staring.

"With the four little ones, Colleen doesn't get to rest or eat like she should. Especially not at this stage." Out of the corner of her eye, she caught the motion of his head shake. "Seems like those kids are always coming down with something. At least this time it was just the flu. Last time it was cholera."

She'd seen the wrenching effects of that terrible disease once while helping her father. The memory turned Claire's stomach. "Poor things."

Bryan released a long sigh. "Yeah. Thomas spends most of his time at the Travona, and I know the girls try to help as much as they can. It's hard."

This was her chance. "What was the breathing mask Mrs. O'Leary mentioned?" She stole a glance at him. "If you don't mind me asking. Or if you'd rather not answer…"

Was that red creeping up to his ears? Or heat from the sun? "I don't mind. Lung conditions are a big problem for the miners, so my brother asked some friends back east to make a mask to filter contaminants from the air as the miners breathe. I just received the first three this week, and Thomas is trying one." A light spread across his face as he spoke. "Hearing that it helps is the best news I've had this month."

Excitement bubbled up in her chest. "That's great. Will you ask them to send more?"

Bryan's mouth pinched. "Yes, certainly. They're not inexpensive, but I'm hoping maybe the mine owners will help offset the cost."

"Do you think they will?"

He glanced at her with a wan smile. "I think it's a vain hope. But I have to try."

They'd reached the café, and Bryan paused at the base of the front stairs. Claire didn't want him to leave. Not yet. Not when they'd finally had their first civil conversation.

"Well…thanks for escorting me. I mean…letting me escort you back." He shifted his doctor's bag from one hand to the other. Was he nervous? Or maybe he didn't want to end the conversation yet, either. The butterflies moved up to her chest.

"Thank you." And then she forced herself to turn away and trudge up the stairs. The warmth of his gaze followed her all the way.

Chapter Ten

"*T*hank you, sirs." Claire slipped the coins in her apron pocket as the last group of miners rose and headed toward the door. Aunt Pearl had left the café early tonight because of a headache. But the patrons were friendly, so the extra work hadn't been a burden. Except now, her feet ached all the way up to her backbone.

She stacked plates as the men shuffled toward the door. The door closed behind them, leaving her to her work. In the stillness, a throat cleared. Claire jerked her head up.

Doc Bryan stood by one of the front tables. He must have slipped in when the others left. He clutched his leather bag and looked as weary and soot-covered as any miner. "I, um… I know it's late. Wasn't sure if you had an extra plate of food left. I can take it with me."

Claire's stomach flipped as she motioned toward the only clean table in the room. "Have a seat. I'm sure I can find you something."

When she ducked back into the kitchen, Lilly was elbow deep in wash water, and Dahlia sat in the corner knocking two wooden blocks together. "Lilly, is there another plate of food left? The doctor's here and looks like he could use it."

The woman nodded toward a cloth draped over the work table. "Under that."

"Thanks."

Claire studied the man as she carried the plate to him. With arms crossed and chin tucked against his chest, he looked asleep. But no. His brown gaze was staring at the table edge. Though she doubted he was interested in the wood.

As she neared, he seemed to come awake. Dropping his hands to his lap, he sent her a smile, but it died at the worry lines around his eyes. What had happened since he'd escorted her back to the café this afternoon?

She placed the plate in front of him. "I think it's still warm. If not, let me know, and I'll reheat it."

Without glancing at the food, he picked up his fork. "Looks wonderful."

She stood there. Watching. She should have been cleaning the rest of the tables and helping Lilly with the dishes. But for some reason, her feet wouldn't move. "Is something wrong?"

He took a bite of green beans and chewed. His eyes focused ahead, each bite methodical, as if it were an effort. "A fire. In the cabbage patch district."

Claire sucked in a breath, wrapped her arms around her waist, and gripped her elbows. "Is everyone all right?"

"One died. Old miner who's been struggling with the lung disease for a while." His expression was stoic, his words emotionless. "Eight homes burned. If you can call 'em that. Shacks, really. Worse than O'Leary's." His face turned to meet hers, and the bleakness in his gaze nearly knocked her to the floor.

"Bryan." She sank into a chair as the word took the last of her air. "What will they do without homes?"

He let a long breath seep out as his elbows rested on the table and his gaze dropped again. "Move in with others for now. Eventually, rebuild the same filthy hovels they lost. It never changes. No matter what I do. How hard I push. It never…changes."

The desolation in his voice nearly reached into her chest and smothered her lungs. She slipped out a hand, resting it flat on the table, just inches from his. Everything in her wanted to touch him. Squeeze the passion back into his veins. "Bryan. The work you're doing helps. You have to see that." Why was she saying this? Hadn't she thought him a sham just weeks ago? But seeing him with the O'Leary family. Listening to work he'd been doing to help the miners. He cared. He may not always let it show, but he cared deeply for his patients.

His gaze reached up and found hers. She struggled to cope with the weight of the burden reflected in his eyes. Wanted to take some of it off him. It was too much for one man.

"Mi' Claire?"

Claire's attention jerked to the source of the little voice. Dahlia. With her dark hair floating in waves around her shoulders, she was adorable enough to make Claire's chest ache more than it already did. "Hi, honey. What are you doing out here?"

But the almost-two-year-old turned toward Bryan and held up her hands in the universal *hold me* sign.

"Honey—" Claire reached for Dahlia so the doctor wouldn't feel uncomfortable, but he'd already scooped her up and perched her on his lap. He scooted his chair back a few more inches from the table's edge.

"Hi, little bit. Bet you'd like a bite of my blackberry pie." He reached for the spoon Claire'd brought for him to use with his corn and sliced off a child-sized bite of the rich burgundy dessert.

Dahlia opened her sparrow mouth, and her eyes grew wide as she closed on the treat.

"Good, huh?"

She bobbed her head dramatically, bringing a smile onto his face. The first real one she'd seen tonight. It lit his eyes from within, taking away some of the roguishness from his expression.

"Have you already tucked Rose into bed?" He offered the question while he loaded another spoonful of pie.

She nodded again. "Sleeping."

He glanced up at Claire, a twinkle flashing. "Rose is a special friend. Came all the way from Raleigh, North Carolina." Turning back to the girl, he slipped the bite into her open mouth. "Miss Claire came from North Carolina, too. Did you know that? Maybe she and Rose met before they both came here?"

The little girl turned to her, eyes still wide. A new appreciation reflected in their depths. "Mi' Claire stay here, too?"

Claire swallowed, willing her throat not to close. "I don't know, honey. I might not be needed much longer." She brushed a wisp of feather-soft hair from the girl's cheek.

She didn't miss the raised brows Bryan shot her way. But she couldn't quite look at him.

"You…don't think you're needed here?" He asked the question directly. The words she'd tried to ignore, now voiced out loud.

She steeled her jaw to keep the tears from reaching her eyes. "Gram's getting married. Did you hear?" Could he tell the cheerfulness took all her effort?

"I…hadn't heard." He was studying her. But once again, she ignored it.

"I understand Mose proposed last night. Gram's going to be riding along on his freight trips after they're married."

He didn't answer. Didn't stop looking at her, until Dahlia grabbed his hand and pulled. "Mo, pease."

He sliced another bite and slid it into the child's mouth, then leveled his gaze on Claire again. "He'll take care of her. Ol' Mose is a good man."

"I know." And she did. Something about Ol' Mose seemed so genuine. No matter how much she wanted to dislike him, she couldn't. How could she object to something that would fill Gram's final years with happiness? What a selfish child she could be.

"It's okay to worry. It's even okay to be sad about the change." Bryan's words soaked through her.

Dahlia had stopped begging for bites and snuggled deeper into the crook of Bryan's arm. He wrapped his free hand around to cup her shoulder, cradling her in his strength.

The two of them were a welcome distraction from the thoughts swirling through her mind.

"I hope..." Bryan stopped, his brows knitting. He didn't meet her gaze.

She almost prompted him but clamped her mouth shut against the words. He'd speak when he was ready.

At last, his voice came softer. "I'm sure your grandmother wouldn't want you to leave right away, even if the wedding's soon." His voice held the tiniest bit of a quiver as he raised his eyes to meet hers. "I imagine Aunt Pearl would like you to stay around, too."

His words hung in the air as she sank deep in his gaze. Did he want her to stay, too? Did she want him to want that? But what kind of crazy thought was that? She didn't even like the man.

Dahlia stirred in Bryan's arms, pulling Claire's attention. Eyes closed, the little flower had fallen asleep, her fist curled up at her mouth in the adorable habit.

Bryan stroked his large hand over the soft curls. "Is there a bed around here I can put her in?"

Claire scanned the room, the sight jerking her back to reality. She still hadn't finished wiping down the tables. And poor Lilly was washing dishes by herself in the kitchen. What in the Great Smokey Mountains had come over her to get lost in this conversation, leaving all her work undone? Claire Sullivan *never* shirked her duties.

Jumping to her feet, she motioned for Bryan to follow. As she held the curtain divider aside for the pair to enter the kitchen, Lilly turned from her position at the sink.

The woman's eyes softened as they landed on the sleeping form of her child. Then they darted from Bryan to Claire, a hint of fear taking over her face. "I am sorry."

She reached for her daughter, but Bryan turned his body to stop the woman. Lilly's troubled eyes sought the doctor's, and Claire found herself doing the same.

"It's okay." Bryan's expression probed into the young mother, and the worry lines around her mouth and eyes finally softened.

"Thank you." She reached again for Dahlia, and Bryan easily handed her over.

"Lilly, take her home now. I'll finish up here." Claire stepped forward, slipping a hand on the woman's shoulders. "I didn't mean to leave you alone with the dishes so long."

Lilly's gaze darted to the sink, where stacks of clean plates and mugs spread across the work counter. "They are washed, I only need to put away."

"I'll do it. Go." Claire applied some pressure and encouraged the woman and child toward the door.

Lilly's eyes found hers and searched. Why was it so hard for her to accept a gift? She seemed to always worry she was imposing or not carrying her weight. When would Lilly see she did more than any of them, preparing and cooking most of the food for the throngs that filled the café dining room?

"Thank you." Lilly's perfect pronunciation of the words came across with a hint of fragility. One day, Lilly would trust her enough to share her story. It must be quite a tale.

As the woman and child left, Claire turned to Bryan. "You haven't even had a chance to eat yet. I'll bring you another slice of pie, too."

The lines around his eyes had deepened, and the hollows underneath grown dark. "Thanks."

After she delivered the new slice, Claire set to work wiping down the tables in the dining room. Bryan didn't speak again.

A couple times, she could feel the weight of his gaze. Once, she even turned to stare back. He didn't drop his focus, just lifted a corner of his mouth in a smile that didn't reach his eyes, then took another bite.

When the tables were clean, Bryan was scraping the last blackberry from his pie plate. "I'll take those dishes for you." She reached to swipe the plates from in front of him.

Bryan raised his eyes to her. "Food hit the spot."

She nodded. "Lilly's a good cook."

His brows crept up. "You and your grandmother made the pie?"

Claire dipped her chin. "Gram's pie crusts are the best."

A twinkle found his eye, but he didn't say more on the subject, just pulled out a coin to pay for the meal. "Sorry to keep you so late. Do you have much more to do?"

Scanning the room, Claire ran through the night duties in her mind. "Not much. I just need to put the dishes away and sweep the floors." She turned back with a nod. "Have a nice evening, Doctor."

Have a nice evening, Doctor. So they were back to that, were they? Did she even know she'd been calling him by his Christian name less than an hour before? Bryan released a long breath and leaned back in the dining chair. It was probably for the best. She was too attractive for them to be alone if she was actually being *nice* to him.

Dishes clanged from the kitchen. She shouldn't have to stay late and clean the cafe by herself because of him.

Memories of the man he'd been unable to save flickered through his mind. And the families who would be homeless tonight. Where were they sleeping? On the rough wooden floors of other shacks? That would be one of the better options. An image of his cot back at the clinic flashed through his mind. It would be luxury to those families.

And yet, he couldn't quite bring himself to go there. The intense loneliness of the room was the very last thing he could face right now.

He glanced at the broom leaning against the wall in the corner. Heaving to his feet, he trudged toward it. It was the least he could do.

Chapter Eleven

Claire pushed through the curtain and slowed her steps at the sight before her. Bryan…holding a broom. Sweeping.

He must have sensed her presence, because he looked up. Was that red creeping higher on his neck? "I'm just finishing in here."

"You… I… I didn't…" She took a deep breath. Aunt Pearl would have a hissy fit if she knew a paying customer was helping clean. She prided herself on the best service in the Montana Territory.

He shrugged. "It was the least I could do." Opening the front door, he swept the pile of dust and food scraps out toward the street. The sound of a male voice drifted through the opening. Bryan answered, but she couldn't distinguish his words. He'd been caught by someone on the street, doing her work.

Claire wanted to slink back into the kitchen, but she stood her ground and faced him with a smile when he reentered. "Thank you."

He paused on the threshold and scanned the room. She followed his gaze. The tables had been straightened, the chairs stacked upside down on their surfaces. Everything in order.

His eyes found hers across the distance. "What next?" Even though he tried to hide it, his shoulders didn't hold their normal straight line. He was bone-tired.

"That's all. I'll lock the door behind you before I head out the back." She stepped toward the front as he picked up his doctor's bag on the edge of the table where he'd eaten.

When she reached the door, she turned, waiting for him to exit. He still stood in the middle of the room, case in hand. "Lock that, and I'll walk out the back with you."

Why did he always make things hard? "It would be easier for you to go out this way." She propped a hand on her hip, resisting the urge to tap her toe.

"I'll see you home. It's too dark in that alley for a woman alone at night."

He wanted to walk her home? If it were any other man making the proposition, she'd refuse and flee his company. But surely she could trust the town doctor. And the way he'd snuggled Dahlia and teased the O'Leary children earlier? Even Lilly seemed to trust the man.

"Okay." She slid the bolt into its metal slot and pivoted toward the kitchen.

After they stepped out the back door, she turned and used the skeleton key. When the lock clicked in place, she spun back and eyed the doctor. The location of the key was a strict secret. Only the three of them were to know. Not even

Jasper, who kept the cafe stocked with firewood each day, knew where Aunt Pearl kept it hidden. "You'll have to look away."

Bryan's chin jerked toward her, but she couldn't see his expression in the shadows. "You have a secret?" Amusement laced his voice.

"Face that direction, please." She pointed toward a house on the other side of the alley.

She half expected him to argue, but he obeyed. She slipped the key in the shrub beside the stoop and spun away from the spot. "All done."

As they strolled down the path toward Gram's house, the crickets sounded their evening greeting. Fireflies danced under an almost-full moon and a vast canvas of stars. Such a beautiful night. Peaceful even.

"My brother, Alex, and his wife enjoyed meeting you the other night. Miriam talks every day about how she's going to make time to come visit you. She stays busy, though."

Claire forced a smile. "I would love her visit, but I seem to stay busy myself. I've enjoyed working at the café, though."

A tenseness seemed to take over the silence. She chanced a glance at him in the moonlight. His dark brows knit together, his lips pinched. Had she said something wrong? Honestly. This man could be so moody sometimes, he didn't make sense.

At last Bryan spoke. "I was surprised you took a job when your purpose in coming was to care for your grandmother."

A flash of anger whipped through her. He was judging her? But maybe he didn't know the situation. How could he. She nibbled her lip. It might look strange to someone looking in from the outside. She could give a few details anyway. Put some perspective on it.

"When I arrived, I quickly found Gram's situation wasn't as...stable...as we'd assumed. My work at the café helps to balance that. And Gram seems to nap most of the time I serve lunch, and comes in to eat dinner most nights, too. And..." She shrugged. "Aunt Pearl needs the help, so it's good for everyone."

"I see." He didn't sound as resentful now, but didn't say anything further. Had she silenced his concerns?

Maybe a change of topic was better. "Is Alex your only brother?" She hadn't meant to ask about his personal life, but the question came out before she realized. Something about this man was intriguing. What formed his reserved exterior? And why did he hide his caring nature underneath? Or was it only certain things that drew out the compassion in him? Like children.

"Alex is my only brother, but we had two sisters. Cathleen still lives at home in Boston."

"Had?" The minute the word left her tongue she wanted to recall it. She nibbled her lip. Should she tell him to ignore the question? Or would that be even more rude?

"Britt died from a lung disorder when she was ten." His voice grew soft, but the pain didn't sound raw.

Still…how hard must it have been to lose a sibling? If anything ever happened to Marcus, he would take a piece of her with him. "Bryan, I can't imagine. I'm so sorry."

"Cathleen's seventeen now and helps Dad in his apothecary's shop. I'm not sure Mum wants her to work, but since Alex and I both left, Dad's determined to pass his legacy on to somebody."

A surge of homesickness washed through Claire. How was Papa doing without her to assist in his clinic? She couldn't think about that now. "Are you the eldest brother then?"

Several beats passed before, as they reached Gram's, he answered. "Yes."

The quiet resignation in the word almost took her breath.

Claire inhaled a steadying breath, squared her shoulders, and pushed open the door to Lanyard's Dry Goods. Fester, the freckled clerk she'd met that first day, was wrapping a purchase for a customer at the counter. He looked up when she strolled forward to wait behind the patron, and the tips of his ears turned red. "Howdy, Miss Sullivan."

"How are you, Mr. Fester?" She turned on her sweetest Southern drawl. Let the man squirm. They should know better than to scam customers the way they had Gram.

The burly woman in front of her gathered her packages and turned to go, offering a polite nod as she passed Claire.

Claire deposited her money on the counter, giving the man a syrupy smile. "Five dollars to pay on Mrs. Malmgren's tab, sir. And a pound of coffee, please. How much will that be?" She waited for the number, and handed over the exact change from her own funds. This was the last of her spending money. After this, she'd be tapping into the resources she needed for her return trip, when Gram no longer needed her to stay. But every bit of her earnings from the café had to go toward getting Gram out from under the ownership of this storekeeper.

With the sack of coffee tucked under her arms, Claire exited the shop and paused on the threshold. Since she was already on that end of town, this would be the perfect chance to check on the O'Learys.

After traipsing the two blocks to the little shanty, Claire knocked. It was answered by the older boy. Was his name Malcom? Both lads shared freckles across their cheeks, but this one's hair was a darker auburn than little Sid's curls.

"Hello. I'm Miss Sullivan. I came by last week. I wanted to see if you're all feeling better."

He nodded, then called over his shoulder. "Mum, the lady with the food's here." Then addressing Claire again, "Nobody's throwed up since yesterday."

Claire didn't try to bite back her smile. "I'm glad to hear it."

Mrs. O'Leary appeared behind the lad. "Malcom, show the lady in." She turned a tired smile to Claire as she gripped her son's shoulder and pulled him and the door to the side. "Come in, Miss Sullivan. You were a godsend the other day. A gift from the Almighty. I was just fixin' ta heat the last of that stew. Won't you sit an' eat with us?" The woman reached under her rounded midsection, as if helping to support it.

Claire followed her into the kitchen. There in a pot on the table sat about a third of the stew she'd brought. How did they still have any left with so many mouths to feed? The children must have been sick indeed. But there wasn't enough here for the family to eat, much less adding her into the mix. "I just ate. Thank you, though."

Mrs. O'Leary bent to pull a crate from under the table, and Claire jumped to help her. "Let me."

"I was gonna add these potatoes into it, too." The woman stepped back and allowed Claire to lift the wooden box to the table top. Mrs. O'Leary seemed to be breathing hard from the effort of leaning down.

Claire softened her voice. "Why don't I slice the potatoes and finish the stew while you go rest. I can keep an eye on the children, too." She glanced around. Malcom sat by the open door, spinning a top with a string. Where were the other three?

"Are you sure?" Mrs. O'Leary looked like she might argue the point, but the exhaustion radiating from her eyes must have overtaken any concerns. "Sid's already nappin', and the girls are playin' at the neighbor's."

"Perfect."

Claire found the same dull knife she'd used the other day and set to work. Malcom seemed to watch her as much as he did his toy. Every time she glanced up at him, he jerked his gaze away.

"You're pretty good at spinning that top." Claire kept her focus on the potato in her hand but watched the boy from the edge of her vision.

His shoulders squared, like a male bird preening. "Just got it fer my birthday, but I'm better'n all the others."

And not a bit proud of it. Claire pursed her lips against a smile. "Are you teaching Sid how to spin it as well as you?"

The boy ducked his head and sent the top spinning again. "I guess."

"You know, that's the most important job an older brother has, learning how to do stuff really well so you can teach the younger ones. I have a big brother, Marcus, and he was the best teacher ever." She finished peeling the potato in her hand and sliced it into chunks.

The boy's brows drew lower as curiosity took over his face. "Did your brother teach you to spin a top?"

"He did. And how to whistle, and fish, and climb trees all the way near the top." Claire picked up another potato to peel. This one had several bad spots that looked like they ran deep. She pressed harder to get to the base of the largest one.

Malcom let loose a low whistle. "Mum won't let Cath and Audrey climb trees."

Claire met his gaze. "I probably shouldn't—"

The knife slipped, slicing into the side of her hand just above the thumb. The force of her effort drove the knife deep, but it took a couple seconds for the burning pain to set in.

"What is it, Miss Sullivan?" Malcom was at her side as Claire gripped her fingers against the sting.

Blood leaked out faster than she would have expected. Claire searched the counter for a cloth. There. The hand towel looked dirty, but it was better than bleeding all over the food.

"What's wrong?" Malcom's voice had an edge of panic.

"I just cut myself." Claire spoke through gritted teeth. Blood soaked through the cloth like water from a spring, and the pain shot through her arm with every pounding in her chest.

"You're bleedin' ever'where. I'm goin' to get, Mum."

"No." The word came out sharper than she meant, and Malcom froze mid-step. "Your Mum needs the rest. Please don't wake her."

The cloth was soaked with blood now. She must have cut an artery. Claire scanned the kitchen from top to bottom as pain pulsed through her hand. Flour sacks lay folded under the counter. She grabbed one and pressed hard against the wound.

A voice from outside drifted through the open door. Where was Malcom? But she couldn't worry about the boy right now. She had to get this wound to stop bleeding.

And then another voice sounded. Deeper. So familiar. Her heartbeat raced even as the tension in her shoulders eased.

Chapter Twelve

*B*ryan leaped up the step into the shack and paused a half second to get his bearings. There. In the kitchen.

The sight of Claire Sullivan with blood streaking her clothes took away the last of his breath. Pain and panic enveloped her face.

Two strides brought him to her. "Let me see it." He reached for the hand she cradled, clasping his palm over the flour sack she used to stem the bleeding. It was pretty well soaked with crimson. He eased the cloth away so he could see the extent of the damage. An inch long slice ran deep in the side of her hand. Must have hit the radialis indicis artery.

Blood had already sprung to the surface of the cut as he examined it, and the liquid ran in rivulets down her hand. He pressed the cloth back to the wound and glanced up to take stock of Claire's other symptoms.

Her face had grown pale. Was that traumatic shock from the wound? Or had she lost enough blood to be experiencing hypovolemic shock? "Let's sit you down on the floor here."

Keeping the pressure steady with one hand, he slipped the other behind her back and eased her down. "Malcom, can you bring me a blanket, lad?"

The boy was by his side within seconds, a quilt in hand.

"Excellent. Slip it under Miss Sullivan's head for now." Should he ask for another to cover her? She wasn't shivering, and no bluish tint showed around her lips. Breathing seemed fairly steady. He pressed two fingers to her neck. Pulse wasn't quite as strong as he'd like, but not racing. Still, her skin was a bit clammy. "Do you have one more?"

As he waited, Bryan's gaze slipped up to Claire's face. She watched him, pain pinching her lips. But her eyes locked in his. Was that trust he saw there?

He brushed the hair from her forehead. "You'll feel better soon."

"I know," she whispered.

Heat flooded his chest. When had he started to care so much about this woman?

"Here, Doc." Malcom knelt on Claire's other side with another quilt.

"Help me spread it over her."

The boy obeyed eagerly, although it took several tries before he had the blanket covering both her legs and abdomen at the same time.

Bryan settled the cover at her chin and couldn't help brushing a thumb over her cheeks. So soft. Cool, with no clamminess.

Her eyes never wavered from his face, and he forced himself to give her a smile. "Let's see if the bleeding's stopped."

Grasping her hand in both of his, he eased the cloth away. Only a few drops of blood pooled at the surface of the cut. Almost ready to stitch.

After finding a single spot on the cloth that wasn't blood-soaked, he reapplied the pressure and reached for his bag. There was no way he'd stitch the wound without giving her something for the pain, although he had a feeling she would object.

"I need you to take a sip of this. Can you hold it while I raise your head?"

Wariness took over her eyes as he held up the brown-tinted glass bottle.

"Please."

She nibbled her lip but finally wiggled her good hand out from under the blanket and reached up for the laudanum. Blood covered the fingers, lay imbedded under her nails, and ran in dry streaks over her palm and down her arm.

"One good sip." Too bad he couldn't measure it out, but he just didn't have enough hands. An approximate dose would be all right.

He slipped his hand into her silky hair to raise her head. The delicate muscles in her neck rippled as she drank.

She sank back against the folded quilt, releasing a long breath as she relaxed.

"Can you keep the pressure on your hand while I ready the sutures?" He watched her for any sign of hesitation, but she merely slipped her hand under his and pressed the cloth.

His skin tingled where her fingers touched his. What was wrong with him? He'd never had a physical reaction to a patient before. Not good. Of course, he'd never had a patient as striking as Claire Sullivan either.

By the time he had his tools laid out and the silk sutures threaded through the needle, Claire's eyes were drifting shut.

"I'll take it now." He pried her fingers from the bloody flour sack and eased the cloth away from the wound. Bleeding had stopped. *Thank you, Lord.* "You'll feel a sting, but try to relax."

"All right." Her delicate eyelids had closed, and the words came out as a relaxed whisper. It must have been hours since she'd last eaten for such a small amount of laudanum to have this much effect. Or maybe she was especially sensitive to the drug.

He cleaned the wound and stitched as quickly as he could. The sooner this was over, the better. When he had a bandage securely in place, he sat back on his heels and started packing the tools. "That should take care of it. Malcom, where's your mum?"

"Takin' a nap with Sid." The boy kneeled at Miss Sullivan's feet, watching the scene with wide eyes.

"I guess we better wake her. I need to get Miss Sullivan home."

Claire grabbed his arm with her good hand. "No. She needs to rest. I'll finish the stew and go home when I'm done."

He couldn't resist brushing the hair back from her cheek. "Relax. You're in worse shape than Mrs. O'Leary at the moment. Let someone care for you this once."

A strange look flickered across her face. Was it his imagination, or did she lean into his hand where it cupped her cheek? The moment stretched as he watched her watch him, their eyes locked.

"Miss Sullivan, what's happened, lass?" Mrs. O'Leary's words broke through their connection, and Claire's hand slipped from his arm.

Bryan leaned back, removing his hand from Claire's cheek. The loss of her warmth left his skin tingling.

"Just had a little accident. I'm sorry about this mess. I'll clean it up in a minute." Claire struggled to sit up, and Bryan eased an arm behind her shoulders to help.

"Easy, there." He gripped her shoulder with a staying hand once she sat straight. "That's far enough."

She'd lost some color in her face with the activity. Given a few minutes, she might regain it. Regardless, no way was he letting her stand up and try to walk out of here on her own.

Bryan's eyes wandered the room as his thoughts drifted through the possibilities. He could get a wagon from the livery. That might be his only real option. His gaze focused on Claire's face. "If we move you to a chair, will you stay there until I return?"

Her pretty forehead puckered. "Bryan, I'll be fine. You don't need to fuss."

He gave her his best doctor-in-charge look. "I know you'll be fine if you're sitting in the chair. You lost a lot of blood, it's going to take your body a few days to spring back."

"Just help me up, and you'll see."

Bryan fought to keep a smile from showing as he helped her rise to her feet. Yes, they'd see.

Claire's face had lost all color by the time she stood upright, and she swayed under his grip on her elbows. He shifted his left arm so it wrapped around her back. If he hadn't been there, she'd have landed flat on the floor again.

"Help me to a chair." She spoke through clenched teeth. Was she angry because he was right? Or struggling that much not to lose consciousness? She was too pitiful for him to gloat.

"Easy, there."

She leaned into him as he helped her to a seat at the table in the corner.

Mrs. O'Leary shuffled behind them, starting to clean up the mess on the floor.

"I'll help you in a moment, Colleen," he called over his shoulder.

"Nonsense. She needs you more. I've had a good rest and need somethin' ta do."

And he could only handle one damsel in distress at a time. Bryan eased Claire into the chair, watching her expression.

She seemed to be holding her breath through the effort, then released it in a long slow leak as she relaxed.

He gathered one of the quilts and tucked it over her lap. "Will you stay here while I go get a wagon? Not try to move?" He searched her eyes for the truth.

She met his gaze, fatigue radiating from those striking eyes.

His chest ached to take away the weariness.

"Yes," she murmured. "Go."

She was too beautiful. His hands craved the feel of her cheek again. He balled his fists to keep them at his side. "I'll be back soon." As soon as he could possibly make it.

The errand turned out to be quicker than he'd expected. He caught sight of Robert Schmidt passing with a delivery from the mercantile, and the man didn't hesitate when Bryan asked for a ride for his patient.

"Sure thing, doc." Robert reined the team to a stop in front of the O'Leary's shanty, and Bryan strode back up the step to gather Claire.

He dropped to one knee in front of her as he peered into her face. She had better color now. "I've found you a ride. Can you walk out to the wagon if I help you?"

"Of course." She turned those bewitching eyes on him, and even in her weakened state, they made his heart seize.

He gripped her elbow as she struggled to her feet.

Colleen O'Leary approached with his doctor's bag, and Claire handed the quilt back to her with a weak smile. "Thank you. I'm sorry for the mess."

"Pshaw." The woman waved the apology aside. "Yer a blessing, lass."

The wagon seat was wide, and as he assisted Claire up into it, she scooted to the middle so he could sit as well. He'd been planning to walk, but...

When he settled onto the bench beside her, Claire inched closer to him. She did know him better than Robert. Still, Bryan was achingly aware of her closeness.

Claire's elbow brushed his arm, and Bryan glanced at her face. Colorless. Was that a tinge of blue around her lips? She looked like she might fall over any second. He reached his left arm behind her for extra support, and she leaned against him. She fit perfectly there. Her head nestled against his shoulder.

She let out a long breath. Good. As long as she relaxed, her body could heal itself.

If only he could get his own racing heartbeat to slow. What was he going to do about his reaction to this woman?

Chapter Thirteen

$\mathcal{B}$ryan tapped on the door of Mrs. Malmgren's cottage the next morning and waited as a shuffling sounded across the wooden floor inside.

The door opened to reveal Mrs. Malmgren. Her milky eyes appeared to stare in the distance, but she held her chin up, senses alert to identify him.

"Hello, ma'am. It's me, Doc Bryan." He spoke quickly so she wouldn't have to ask.

A smile spread over her face before he finished the *ma'am*.

"Well my goodness, Doctor. Come in, come in. We just put more loaves in the oven an' was sittin' down for coffee."

Bryan peered inside as the woman shuffled toward the table. Claire stood at the wash sink in the kitchen, one hand deep in a basin of water. What was she doing up and working this morning? He'd told her to rest today. No working for Pearl. No wandering about town helping neighbors.

He was three strides into the room before he stopped himself. *Calm down, man. You're over-eager.*

"Good morning." The soft voice from the sink focused his attention on the woman. It was hard to tell from the dim light whether her color was better or not, but a soft smile lit her features.

"Morning."

She was beautiful. The white apron strings gathered into a bow at her waist, the loops almost longer than her slender figure. Something was different with her hair today. She'd pinned it up, not tied it back in a loose ribbon like yesterday. As much as he loved that hair, this look accentuated the length and curve of her neck. Stunning...to put it mildly.

A noise to his right pulled Bryan's attention. Mrs. Malmgren settled into a chair at the table, the wooden legs scraping the floor. She leaned back, a smile quirking her mouth. "I guess you came to check on our Clara Lee."

Bryan darted a glance at Claire as he cleared his throat. "Yes, ma'am."

"I don't guess we're used to so much personal service 'round here." The older woman's voice teased. Bryan tried to ignore it, but the heat crept up his neck anyway.

Claire turned from the sink, wiping the fingers of her good hand on her apron. "I'm much better now. Thanks for checking, though. Would you like coffee?"

"Yes, I suppose so. Thanks." Bryan glanced from Claire to her grandmother. What did he do now? More than anything, he'd needed to rest his eyes on the woman and know she was recovering from the loss of blood. Maybe if he played along with the coffee, she'd give him the chance to... To what? Examine her hand? Talk?

Claire approached the stove and held her hand about six inches over the top surface. Only the side of her face was visible from where he stood, but the frown was clear.

She bent and reached for a log from the stack beside the cook stove. With a rag over the handle, she stepped back as far as she possibly could while still gripping the knob. Nudging the handle up, she released the door to the fire box and swung it wide. Her head turned to the side, eyes squinted shut, as she threw the log into the fire and slammed the iron door shut.

Bryan strode to her side and rested a hand on her shoulder. "Are you hurt? Smoke in your eyes?"

She exhaled a long breath, then opened her eyes and straightened. "I'm fine."

But she wasn't. Her face had gone pale as newly fallen snow. "Are you light-headed? Come sit in a chair." He gripped her elbow to assist, but she jerked it back.

"I'm all right. Really. I just...don't like fire." She spun away and marched to the work counter.

He stared at her back. *Didn't like fire?* He didn't like radishes, but he didn't go ashen when he had to look at them.

He eyed the stove. "Do you want me to add another piece of wood?"

"If you'd like." But there was a hint of relief in her voice.

He loaded two logs into the fire box, then closed the door and locked the handle in place. After moving the coffee pot to the front of the stove, he turned back to watch Claire again.

She picked up a used plate from in front of Mrs. Malmgren and carried it to the wash bucket in the sink. Her steps seemed sturdier, her color much improved.

Mrs. Malmgren seemed to know he was watching her. "Why don't you two young'uns take your coffee to the porch? It's such a pretty day, an' the light's better out there so you can see to put more salve on Clara Lee's hand."

Claire twisted to look at her. "Do you want to come out with us, Gram? We can bring another chair."

"No, honey. I think I might walk next door an' see how Mrs. Walker's gettin' on."

Was the older woman doing some matchmaking? Interesting.

Claire gathered the coffee pot from the stove and filled two mugs. She handed him one.

His work kept him too busy to think about courting anyway. Sure, Alex had done it. But there was more Bryan still wanted to do to help the miners. So many lives left to save. Paying court to a woman would just distract his focus. In fact, he should be out at the mines already. Just a few more minutes here, then he'd head to The Original.

"You coming?" Claire stood in the open doorway, her face shadowed as the morning light framed her silhouette.

"Yes." A few minutes to redress her bandage wouldn't hurt anything.

Mrs. Malmgren followed him out, using her cane to feel for the steps, then gripping the rail to assist her down. "I'll be back after a good visit, unless she's not home," she called over her shoulder. "Clara Lee, don't forget about the bread in the oven."

"I'll get it, Gram. Enjoy yourself."

Bryan studied the twin furrows between Claire's brows, then followed her gaze to her grandmother. "She gets around well."

It was several moments before Claire answered. "There are just so many ways she can get hurt."

A memory flashed through his mind. Her grandmother had been burned that first time he'd met her. Hadn't it been from a fire at that very cook stove? He hesitated. Should he press the issue? Finally, he asked the question. "You're worried she'll burn herself again?"

Her shoulders tensed. "That and everything else."

Something about fire seemed to hit a nerve with her. Best to leave that topic alone. But should he address the *everything else*? Remind her she had to allow her grandmother a modicum of independence?

Claire released a sigh. "I know. I need to let her have a little freedom." She turned those piercing brown eyes on him. "I'm trying."

Bryan swallowed. How had she read his mind so completely? He motioned to the rocking chairs. "Do you want to sit?"

He waited for her to settle into the nearest, coffee mug curled in her good right hand. Then he settled in the other chair and sipped his own coffee. "This is good."

A smile touched her lips. "I keep wishing we had milk to make it even better."

"I see you like the finer things in life." He couldn't resist the goading. Although the last thing he wanted to do was awaken her snippy side.

A half-chuckle drifted from her, light and airy, easing Bryan's muscles even as he strained to hear more. "We have a milk cow back home, and she's a great milker. Seems like we're always trying to use up the milk before it spoils."

He allowed his own grin to leak out. "Practical, then."

An easy quiet settled over them as they sipped coffee. He should get on with refreshing her bandage, but... In a minute.

"I plan to make an extra pie this morning and take it to visit your sister between the lunch and dinner crowds."

He raised a brow at her. "She'd love that. You don't have to take food to be welcome, though."

Pink seeped into her cheeks. "I know, but she probably doesn't get much time to bake, working at the clinic and all."

Bryan snapped his fingers. "Actually, she's home today. Her brother and sister-in-law have come down from their ranch in the mountains, so she's home visiting." He lowered his brows to a wry grin. "Miriam and Leah are thick as thieves."

Something flashed through Claire's eyes. Longing? It disappeared before he could be sure. "I won't bother them today, then."

He leaned forward in the chair. "No, this is the perfect time. If you feel up to it, I mean." What was he doing telling her to make house calls when she should be in bed resting? "I mean, you'd like Leah. She and Gideon are the reason I'm here in Butte. They outfitted the clinic and sent a letter to the president at my school inquiring whether a doctor from my graduating class would be interested in coming to Butte." He eased back in his chair. "I guess they figured a younger man would be more willing to come this far away from the civilized East."

Claire tilted her head as she studied him. "Sounds like a smart woman. I'd like to meet this lady."

He nodded, keeping his focus on the mountains in the distance. "Gideon told me last night they've sent for a minister, too. The little church has been empty for a year and a half now."

"Really?" A decided interest crept into her voice. "Did I tell you my brother Marcus is studying to be a minister?"

He glanced over. The pride that filled her voice shown in her face. "Good for him. Does he know what church he'll be going to?"

Melancholy took over her features as her pretty brows gathered. "He just graduated, I think. The ceremony was to take place while I journeyed here."

Bryan wanted to reach up and stroke away the sadness. "I'm sorry."

She blinked, her full lips pinching. He struggled for something else to say. Something to ease the ache so obvious.

Claire broke the quiet as she held out her injured hand. "Would you like to check it now?"

Yes. Doctoring, he could do. Bryan placed his empty mug on the floor beside his chair, then pulled the supplies he'd need from his bag. "Let's have a look."

Claire studied Bryan from the corner of her eye as he examined the stitches on the side of her palm. He was so much more handsome than she'd thought that first day. His strong jaw, those piercing green eyes, every one of his masculine features crafted the most attractive man she'd ever met.

But that was crazy thinking. Her future wasn't here, but his was. She'd come to this territory to help Gram. And soon, Gram would be married, and there'd be nothing left for Claire to do. Except pay off Gram's bill at the dry goods store. Then go back home.

But what then? Help Pa with his medical practice? Plan another benefit for the Charlotte Ladies Aid Society? It all seemed so dull, so routine compared to every moment in these beautiful Montana mountains.

Compared to this moment…with this man. She swallowed to bring moisture back in her throat.

Bryan glanced up and gave her an off-kilter smile. He reached for a clean bandage and the salve. Had he read her thoughts? *Lord, no.* Heat flooded her face.

"Did I tell you we have a new dentist in town?" His baritone drawled like one of the old men playing checkers back home.

Claire blinked, trying to catch up with the topic so very different than her thoughts. "A dentist?"

"Mm-hm." He caught his tongue between his teeth as he tied off the bandage.

"Will that be bad for your business? You know, competition?"

He looked up with an earnestness that clenched her chest. "Not at all. We have more work than Alex and I can handle. Unfortunately. And dental work is…a specialty." He cocked his head. "I just hope the man knows what he's doing."

A rich, yeasty scent drifted on the breeze, tugging at Claire's senses. "My bread." She jumped to her feet and lunged toward the door.

The top surface of the loaves was a darker brown than she would have liked, but not officially burnt. She loosened the bread from the sides of the pans and emptied them onto the counter, then refilled the metal tins with the dough for the last four loaves.

After she slid them into the oven, she turned and offered Bryan a smile. "Sorry about that. Would you like a slice of warm bread? I think we may have a smidgeon of blackberry jam left."

His eyes lit like Marcus' had as a boy opening birthday gifts. "Sure."

Claire turned away to hide her grin at his reaction. She pulled a knife from the jar where Gram kept them, and positioned it over the bread.

"Wait." The command made her jump, and Bryan was by her side in less than a second. One of his hands cupped her shoulder while the other tried to extract the knife from her grip. "I'll do it."

Part of her wanted to sink her elbow in his side, but the rest of her couldn't help a smile as a warm, fuzzy feeling crept into her chest. He was trying to protect her. "I can do it, you know." It wouldn't be fun to give in too easily.

"Humor me this once." He was so close, one arm practically around her shoulders and the other hand covering hers on the knife handle.

She chanced a sideways glance at his face. And froze. Her breath stopped as her gaze locked with his, falling into the depth of those eyes. Normally more green, they'd darkened to almost the richness of coffee.

His breath caressed her face. At least *he* could breathe. His hand slid from her shoulder down to her waist. She turned into him, resting her hands on his chest, as he lowered his mouth to hers.

Sweet mercy. She was lost the moment he connected. Who would have thought a kiss could consume every part of her…so completely?

Chapter Fourteen

Sweet maple sugar. Bryan savored the richness of her, running his hands up her arms, into her hair. She poured passion into her kiss the same way she did every other part of life. So much better than he'd dreamed.

She released a little moan, and it surged through him. He had to get control, or he was going to lose himself completely.

With every ounce of his strength, he tore himself away. At least a few inches, as his forehead dropped to rest on hers. She seemed to struggle for air as much as he.

He slid his palms down to cup her face. "You're beautiful." His chest ached just watching her. His body held strong to the memory of that kiss. Too strong to apologize for it just yet.

"Bryan." His name came from her in a breathy whisper. Good or bad, it was more than he could stand. He went back for another kiss, this one slow and lingering.

When he finally pulled away, he held her close, one hand at the small of her back, the other cupping her cheek. Her face was still upturned to him. As her eyelids fluttered open, they held a dreamy, unfocused look. Her parted lips were plump from the rush of blood. Tempting. So tempting.

His gaze wandered back up to her eyes, starting to sharpen now. "I should probably apologize."

One of those beautiful eyebrows lifted. "You should?"

His mouth pulled in a grin. "I'd rather not."

Her chest rose and fell in what might have been a mind-clearing breath. Then she stepped back. "I, um… I'll get the jam if you want to slice the bread."

He had to blink. Bread. *Right.* Bryan sawed three slices from the loaf. He needed to say something to ease the awareness sparking between them. "At least I didn't let you hurt yourself with the knife."

She had no visible reaction to his words, just reached down to pull two plates and a spoon from a lower shelf. With deliberation, she straightened and turned to face him squarely. Her lips pursed, but a twinkle flashed in her eye. "Your methods, sir, are suspect."

Bryan didn't even try to hold back his grin. He was going to like getting to know this woman.

"Here you go, gentlemen. You won't find a better beefsteak anywhere in the territory." Claire passed out each of the four plates from the tray propped in her left hand.

"Nor a prettier server."

Claire raised a brow at the man to hide the heat crawling up her neck. "Now, Mr. Lincoln."

The town's wiry postmaster raised a hand in defense, ducking behind it. "No offense intended, Miss Sullivan. Just statin' facts."

Mr. Hauswirth elbowed the man in the ribs. "Hush, Frank. Let the woman serve the food."

Claire chuckled as she scanned the table. "Just call if there's anything else you need." Mr. Lincoln nodded through a mouthful of steak and potatoes, and one of the men across from him raised a thumb in the "all's well" sign as he stuffed a biscuit between his jaws.

The bell at the door jingled, and Claire turned with her empty tray to greet the newcomer. She'd not seen the man before, so she gave him a pleasant smile and her official greeting. "Welcome to Aunt Pearl's Café, sir. Take a seat wherever you'd like."

The man removed his hat with a nod. "Thank you."

Claire ducked behind the curtain into the kitchen and set her tray on the counter beside the stove. "Do we have more coffee ready?"

"You can take these two." Aunt Pearl stepped away from the stove to allow access to the pitchers. "You need the tray refilled, too?"

"Just one plate for now. A new man I haven't seen before." Claire grasped the handles of the two coffee pots by the towels tied around them and backed away.

"A miner?"

"Looked like a businessman."

"Don't have time to introduce myself." Pearl poured gravy over the plate of beefsteak in her hand. Lilly and Dahlia were both feeling poorly today, so Aunt Pearl had told them not to come back after the lunch meal. Lilly's quick efficiency was sorely missed tonight, though. And keeping up with the patrons really did take three sets of hands. How had Pearl and Lilly managed for so long with only the two of them?

"Let me pour coffee, and I'll come back for his plate."

As she filled the stranger's coffee cup, Claire tried not to stare at the man's curled handle-bar mustache. "Supper tonight is beefsteak and mashed potatoes with gravy and a biscuit. Aunt Pearl makes the best beefsteak in the territory. She's filling your plate, so I'll have it out shortly."

"Thank you, Miss…" He waited for her to fill in her name.

"Sullivan, sir." She bobbed a curtsey.

The man nodded. "Miss Sullivan. I'm Doctor J. W. Beal. I'll be opening a dental clinic here in town."

Claire stepped back as excitement surged. "I heard there was a new dentist in town. That's excellent." She barely bit her tongue before she asked if he was any good. Truly, she needed to focus on thinking before she spoke.

Humor touched the man's eyes. "I'm glad you think so. I hope the other townspeople feel the same."

Claire backed away from the table. "I'll be back with your plate shortly." She stopped to refill coffee mugs at two tables before returning to the kitchen. The bell jingled, and she looked up.

Bryan. Her chest thumped as butterflies flitted in her stomach.

His gaze found hers, and a grin spread across his face. He turned his steps toward her, and Claire could do nothing but stand in the middle of the aisle and watch him approach. He was so handsome.

For a moment, it looked like he might step close and kiss her. Her heart beat faster.

But he stopped a couple feet away, his gaze hovering on her face. "Good evening."

"Good evening." She couldn't have said how long they stood there, staring at each other.

"Howdy, Doc." The greeting forced its way through the fuzz in Claire's mind.

Bryan glanced behind her. "Hello, Simon. How's the hotel doin'?"

"Just fine. Had to get outta there for some quiet, though."

A smile touched Bryan's face and he turned back to her. "Do you have an extra plate left?"

The words jolted Claire. "Of course. Have a seat." The poor man had come to eat and she'd kept him standing in the aisle. "There's a table in the corner, or..." She stepped closer and dropped her voice to a whisper. "Our new dentist is sitting right there." She nodded toward the man sipping coffee.

Bryan raised both brows at her. "Guess I should introduce myself." As he turned toward the man, Bryan cupped her elbow, brushing his thumb across her upper arm for a quick moment. It was a simple gesture, but the contact sent a skitter of bumps up her shoulder.

Scurrying back to the kitchen, she gathered two plates and a clean mug on her tray. When she reentered the dining room, Bryan sat across from Mr. Beal. The two chatted easily as she approached.

"I've been at Alder Gulch for the last ten years or so," the dentist was saying. "I've missed a larger town, though. The way they say Butte's growing, I imagine it'll be quite a city in a few more years."

Bryan glanced up with a soft smile as Claire filled his mug. "Harris, the superintendent of The Anaconda, came by way of Alder. And Lockton from The Original. Is the gold still flowing there the way it did in the sixties?"

As the dentist responded, Claire slipped away. She didn't often see this side of Bryan. The part of him who was comfortable debating with any businessman. Who not only knew the names of the most influential men in town, but knew the men personally. Knew their stories.

With Bryan so near, it was hard to keep her focus on work, but the demands of the coming and going patrons soon had her scurrying.

Both Bryan and Mr. Beal had finished eating when she made it back to their table to refill coffee mugs. "Are you ready for dessert?"

Mr. Beal leaned his tall frame back in the chair. "None for me tonight. The food was as good as you said, though."

"Thank you, sir." She smiled politely and turned to Bryan.

His gaze dripped with remorse. "I'd better not. Need to stop by Alex's before it gets too late."

"Another time then." Or maybe she could wrap a piece for him to take. Surprise him with it.

After thanking them both, she scurried back to the kitchen and prepared a generous slice of the pecan pie.

"I can do that for ya." Aunt Pearl turned from the sink where she was elbow deep in wash water.

"I've got it. Doc Bryan doesn't have time to stay for dessert, so I'm sending a piece with him." She glanced up to make sure Aunt Pearl was fine with the idea.

The woman bobbed her head. "Good."

When Claire pushed through the curtain doorway, her eyes landed on the table where the doctors sat. Empty. She scanned the room. Bryan wasn't there. The front door was just closing, however, and she sprang forward. Maybe she could catch him on the porch.

As she charged through the door, the two men on the porch stopped conversing and turned to her. Oops. She hadn't meant to be quite so eager. "Sorry, I...was trying to catch Doc Bryan."

Doctor Beal tipped his hat. "I'll take my leave then. And thanks for the information, Doctor Donaghue."

They both watched the dentist descend the stairs and stride down the quiet street.

"Seems like a decent fellow." Bryan's deep baritone merged with the sounds of the crickets.

"I'm glad." She held out the bundle in her hands. "I wrapped a slice of pie for you to take. It's pecan."

One of his long steps brought him closer, a few feet separating them. "Thanks." A smile laced his voice, but shadows hid his face. "I was pretty disappointed I wouldn't get a piece."

As he took the package, his fingers brushed the side of her hand, shooting warmth up to her elbow.

"Claire?" The uncertainty in his voice grabbed her attention. She searched out his gaze, but the darkness made him impossible to read.

"Yes."

"Would you...like to go for a ride with me on Sunday? We could take a wagon and see some of the prettier views in the mountains or..." His brows furrowed. "Do you know how to ride horseback?"

Claire's heart sped, and her head seemed to lose half its weight. "I love to ride and..." She stopped to inhale a deep breath. *Cool it, Sullivan.* "I would enjoy seeing the mountains." Her mind ran through the coming Lord's day. "I have to serve lunch, but the café's closed for dinner, so I could leave right after."

A flash of his white teeth showed in the darkness. "Good."

He stood quietly for a moment. What was he thinking? Did he remember their kiss? The memory still lingered in all of her senses. Did he want to repeat it?

The sound of male voices drifted on the breeze. They came from the direction of Main Street and grew louder. Claire's shoulders sagged. No privacy now.

Bryan stepped back as the men meandered into sight. "I'd better go."

Claire tried to force a smile, even though he probably couldn't see it. "All right."

As Bryan strode down the stairs, he passed the newcomers on the street. His polite "Gentlemen" drifted through the night air, and she couldn't help but cling to the sound as she watched him walk away.

Sunday was just two days away. It couldn't come soon enough.

Chapter Fifteen

Bryan rubbed his damp palms against the sides of his jacket. Even in Montana, men shouldn't be expected to wear a suit and tie in the middle of July. He clenched his fist to keep from tugging at the knotted string around his neck.

What would the men think of his proposal? These three mine owners held the fate of three quarters of the miners in the grip of their whim. Would they hear him out? It'd been a near act of God to get the three of them to meet with him. Together.

But maybe that hadn't been wise. Peer pressure could work against him just as easily as for him. Should he talk about the cost of the masks right away? Or wait until they asked? Forthrightness had always been his policy. Showed men you weren't hiding things.

The door opened and an older woman wearing an apron stepped out. "The gentlemen will see you now, Doctor."

He picked up the breathing mask and pushed to his feet. "Thank you, Miss Percy."

The woman's smile shone across her ebony face as he passed by her through the doorway. "You keep yer chin up, Doc Bryan. You's doin' a good thing."

The whispered words sent a warmth through his chest. Miss Genevieve Percy was one of the most big-hearted women he'd ever met. Martin Daly better know what kind of gem he had in her.

Bryan strode across the large parlor to greet the men seated around a long, low table. They stood to shake hands with him. One would never know by watching the group they were fierce competitors.

When they'd settled back in seats, Martin held up a brandy glass. "What's your drink, Doctor?"

Bryan scanned the various bottles and decanters on the tray beside the man. He had to take something. There, a silver coffee urn. "Coffee. Thanks."

While Martin poured, the other men turned their full attention to Bryan. Best get started. "I appreciate the three of you meeting with me."

William Clark nodded. "You said it was important to the health of our workers." He spread one hand wide. "So, naturally, we're interested." Clark was too much of a politician to make everything he said believable, but that might be a card Bryan could use. The man would want to keep up the appearance of goodwill toward his men.

Bryan leaned forward and rested his elbows on his knees, his eyes roaming to hold each man's gaze as he spoke.

"The men working in the mines have been suffering from an increasing amount of lung conditions. Usually showing as congestion that worsens over time, then develops into fever and frailty a few weeks before they die. So far, this has been the cause of death for at least thirty men over the past year."

He paused for breath and to let that sink in. "I'm currently treating hundreds more for the same symptoms, all suffering in various stages of the disease."

Daly rested his drink on his knee, the lines deepening across his broad forehead. "What do you think is causing the illness?"

"I think it's something they're breathing in the mines. It may simply be lack of quality air. Or might be a component in the dust that coats everything down there."

"Are you seeing it more in any particular trade? The blasters, perhaps?" Martin sounded as if he really cared.

"No." Bryan thought through the jobs of the men who were especially sick. "It's not constrained to the men working with explosives. I've seen it across all trades, I think."

Augustus Heinze crossed his arms over his chest. He had a reputation as the more tight-fisted of the group. "So what is it you think we can do about that?"

Bryan inhaled a fortifying breath, then picked up the mask from beside his feet. "I've been corresponding with some physician friends back East who create medical tools. They've made a breathing mask to filter the air the men take in."

He showed them how the filter worked, and where the spent air released. "I've had three miners try them for the last several weeks." He leveled his gaze on Martin. "Their lung capacity is already better, their congestion lessened. I'm hopeful if they keep wearing the masks, the damage done to their lungs can be reversed."

Clark spoke up, his overgrown brows raised. "You really think that's possible?"

Bryan met his stare. "At the least, we can stop further harm. We can save lives. Your men can work harder and faster when they don't have to stop and catch their breath all day." If only he could tell them the true conditions of some of the sickest men. How they could barely stand, much less work. Yet they still showed up at the mines day after day. But would they be upset to hear some of the men weren't pulling their weight on the job? And there was no way he could tell the stories without making it a personal attack on these mine owners sitting before him. How could they possibly let men work in that condition?

"And I suppose you want us to pay for masks for everyone?" Heinze crossed one leg over the other and slouched in his chair. With his arms still braced over his chest, it was clear he had already made a decision.

"My friends are willing to send them for barely above the cost of supplies and shipping. They're physicians by training, and they want to see the miners helped. It will take some time to manufacture enough for all the men, but—"

"Are there any other options besides the breathing masks?" Daly again. His interest had to be a good sign.

"Anything that would get the men out of the contaminated air." Bryan shrugged. "Breaks through the day where the workers could come to the surface would be best, but it'd be too hard for them to ride the elevators so many times."

"Wouldn't get any work out of 'em," Heinze muttered under his breath.

Bryan did his best to ignore him and focus on Martin and Clark. "It might help if they had shorter work days, where the men could spend time in the sun. I'm not sure yet if lack of sunlight is a contributing factor."

Clark's lips pinched and his brows furrowed. Shorter work days didn't seem to be an idea he liked. Best get back to the more plausible option. "I can order another crate of masks to let more men test them. But I think we should act soon. The men grow worse every day."

Martin sat up, seeming to come awake from his thoughts. He glanced at the other two men. "Well, gentlemen. I'm sure you'll join me in thanking the doctor for his most enlightening conversation."

Bryan sank back into his chair. Ten minutes. Less than a quarter hour to plead his case. Would it make any difference?

As Bryan left the Daly house, the conversation replayed itself in his mind. Had he said enough? Said too much? Maybe he should have told individual stories of some of the men. Tad Langely, who went crazy from grief after his older brother died of the lung disease. That was a cautionary tale if there ever was one. Tad had focused his grief on

Alex's inability to save Tad's brother's life. He'd kidnapped Alex and Miriam to make them suffer a slow, torturous death like his brother had. It was only by the grace of God and Tad's own weakened state that Alex and Miriam had escaped.

How many more people would suffer such grief as they lost loved ones to the mines' angel of death?

A wagon passed near Bryan, and he stepped to the side. He glanced around to get his bearings. Ottawa Street. Claire's grandmother's house stood just two doors further. Why had he come this way? The clinic was two streets over on Elm.

Bryan glanced at the sun. Mid-afternoon. Claire might be between shifts at the café. Would she be home or out on one of her missions of mercy? Did he really want to stop by? Yes. But what excuse did he have for a visit?

The door of her house opened, and the focus of his thoughts stepped out onto the porch with a broom. As she turned, her eyes swept the street...and landed on him. He was close enough to see them widen, then light as a smile spread across her face.

His feet pushed forward, carrying him to the bottom of the steps.

"What are you doing here?" Her smile turned to curious pleasure.

He raised his brows. "I'm not allowed to visit patients?"

The pink in her cheeks was the perfect highlight to her dark eyes. "Of course. I mean…" So cute when she was flustered.

Finally, she stepped back, motioning toward the door. "Would you like to come in? I just pulled cherry pies from the oven."

Normally, that would have started his taste buds going. But his stomach still roiled from the intensity of the meeting. What he really wanted was this woman's company. "Thanks."

He followed her into the house and glanced around. "Where's your grandmother?" And then he heard the soft rise and fall of snoring from the bed chamber.

His eyes found Claire's, and she smiled with a nod. "Her afternoon nap." She motioned toward a chair. "Have a seat while I cut the pie."

"Maybe hold off on the pie for now."

Her gaze flew to his face, searching. "What's wrong?"

Now he was stuck. But a thread of relief eased the weight on his shoulders. It would be nice to have someone to talk to. But would she care about his concerns for the miners? Would she think he was trying too hard? Not hard enough?

"Come sit down." She touched his arm, reining in his thoughts. A line creased her forehead.

He sank into a chair at the table, and she settled into the one catty-corner from his. She leaned forward on her elbows, waiting.

How did he start? Bryan took in a deep breath. "I had a meeting today. With three of the largest mine owners. I proposed some changes."

"And...?"

"You should see the conditions the miners have to work in." The words poured out of him as he described the situations. All those faces he'd treated, the pain in their every breath. For once, he had the chance to share his struggles, his fears for the men. He told of his hopes for the masks. His concern that greed would overcome the chance for this lasting help.

She shook her head. "You can't think they would refuse to buy a tool that could save the lives of their workers. Especially with all that profit."

Bryan cringed. When she put it like that... "I should have had *you* talk to the owners today."

Claire leaned forward and gripped his arm. "I'll do anything to help."

His mouth found a small smile. Her passion flamed like fire in those dark chocolate eyes. Must be the hint of auburn still in her hair, leftover from the Irish roots of her Sullivan name. "I think they need a few days to think through what I told them. Daly seemed like he might be open to the idea. And he owns the largest mine."

Claire sank back into her chair as she released a breath. "I'm so glad you talked to them. I'm glad you're *doing* something."

An ache formed in his chest. Seemed like he'd been *doing* something to help others since he was a boy, but it was never enough.

A muffled clatter sounded behind him, and Bryan turned as Mrs. Malmgren shuffled from the bed chamber.

"Doc Bryan stopped by to visit, Gram." Claire rose and stepped to the cook stove. "I'll pour us all some coffee."

Bryan stood and stepped away from his chair. He'd seen the older woman take that seat at the table before. "How are you today, ma'am?"

"Tickled as a hoppy toad now that you're here, son. Clara Lee, have you cut him some pie?"

Bryan spoke up before Claire could do her bidding. "I'm afraid I need to be leaving. I've a few house calls to make before it gets too late."

A knock rapped on the door.

Silence spread over the three of them, and Claire tilted her head as if she were trying to calculate who it could be.

"Reckon' who it is?" Mrs. Malmgren said in a loud whisper.

Should he answer the door? Hair on the back of Bryan's neck stood on end as he glanced at the thin wooden divider. Slim protection for two women if anyone dangerous did try to come in.

Claire had already stepped to open the door, and Bryan was behind her before his senses kicked in. She opened it a crack and peered around the edge. Then with a jerk, she flung the door open and threw herself in the arms of the man on the porch.

Chapter Sixteen

$\mathcal{B}$ryan's chest seized. It took all his self-control not to reach out to pull Claire back.

"Marcus. What in the world are you doing here?"

Marcus. The name had such a familiar ring. Bryan peered closer at the man's grinning face as he awkwardly patted Claire's back. Her brother? There was a definite resemblance between them. The same dark, piercing eyes. Almost the same hair color, although the man's was a little darker brown.

Claire stepped back, still clutching the man's arm. "Come meet everyone. Of course you remember Gram."

"Is that my Marcus?" Mrs. Malmgren's voice quivered as she reached out a hand.

Marcus stepped forward and clasped it. "Gram, you're a sight for sore eyes." His voice had a relaxed drawl to it. He hugged the older woman, towering over her, but the grin on his face brimmed with affection.

At last, the man's eyes found Bryan. Searching. Taking his measure.

"Marcus, this is Doctor Bryan Donaghue. He's been helping Gram." Claire stood in the space between them. Looking as if she didn't know which man to side with.

Bryan's chest tightened. This shouldn't be hard on her. Her brother had come, it was a happy day. He stepped forward and extended a hand. "It's good to meet you. Claire's talked a lot about you." Too late, he realized he should have said *Miss Sullivan*.

Marcus' grip was firm, and he met Bryan's gaze, raising one brow higher than the other. Then he shifted his focus to Claire. "I hope she hasn't told you any incriminating stories."

"Not yet." Claire stepped closer and slipped her arm through her brother's. "So what are you doing? Please tell me you didn't come all this way just to check on me." She rolled her eyes to Bryan. "Marcus can give a whole new meaning to *overprotective*."

"As if you don't need it." He gave a playful punch to his sister's arm. "But that's actually not the main reason I came." He stood a little straighter. "I've taken a church here in Butte."

Claire sucked in a breath, then let out a little squeal. "You have? Oh, Marcus, that's wonderful." She threw her arms around his waist again.

The grin on Marcus's face was a bit off-kilter as he patted her back and glanced at Bryan. His gaze said he didn't quite know what to do when his sister embarrassed him like this.

"Congratulations," Bryan offered. So this was the new preacher Gideon had sent for? Claire sure seemed to be excited about that fact. What would this do to his chances with Claire? What if Marcus didn't approve of him? Would he try to come between them? How had this woman become so important to him?

Marcus nodded and held his sister at arm's length. "So tell me, how are the two of you doing?" His eyes roamed between her and their grandmother, then zeroed in on the older woman's still bandaged hand. "Is Claire not taking good care of you, Gram?"

His tone was teasing, and Claire gave him a playful swat. "That happened before I got here, thank you very much."

Her own bandage caught his glance and he snatched her wrist, holding it up as his brows lowered. "And you, too? What's going on around here?" His gaze roamed over Claire, then cut to Bryan. Accusing?

Claire pulled her wrist away, and elbowed him with her good arm. "Just a little cut from cooking. Not half as bad as the scrapes you come home with."

Marcus's expression softened as he watched his baby sister.

Claire had a way with him, and it was cute to watch the two of them bicker. Bryan had known they were close, just by the pride in Claire's voice when she talked about her big brother. But the sheer joy on her face now that he was here…

His chest ached. If only he could be the one to put that expression there. At least she had her brother. And he knew all about being overshadowed by a brother. Seemed it was time for him to bow out.

Bryan edged toward the door. "I need to be leaving."

Claire pulled away from her brother and took a tentative step toward Bryan. "Are you sure? Don't you want to stay for pie?" Her eyes said she was sorry their conversation had been interrupted. Her eyes… Windows to her soul. Revealing the purity there.

It made his chest pull even tighter. If only he could step forward, brush his fingers across her cheek. But not with her brother eyeing the two of them.

He swallowed. "I need to get back to the clinic." And bury himself in work. She needed space and time with her brother.

"All right."

As Bryan stepped outside and closed the door behind him, he couldn't shake the feeling his relationship with Claire had just changed.

It was too good to be true.

Claire fought the urge to grip Marcus's arm again. "Come and sit down while I cut us all some cherry pie."

Marcus's face took on that silly grin she remembered from forever. "Cherry pie?"

Warmth flooded her chest. "Sit down. Both of you."

Gram peppered the boy with questions while they settled into chairs around the table. Marcus filled them in on his graduation from seminary and how Dad had heard through one of his contacts in Richmond that Butte was looking for a pastor.

"So here I am." Marcus leaned back and spread his hands, palms up.

"But how did you get here so soon?" Claire slid loaded plates in front of them both and settled down across from her brother. "You still had three weeks before graduation when I left to come here."

He wrinkled his nose at her. "I took a faster boat than you."

It was too good to see him to get riled. "So that's it? You're here for good? Where's all your stuff?" She glanced at the door. He'd not come in carrying anything.

"I agreed to a trial period. Six weeks of sermons, then we'll talk and make sure they like me." He gave a quick, rueful raise of his brows.

"They'll love you." Claire leaned forward on her elbows. "Is your first sermon tomorrow?"

"Next week. When I get settled, I'm to check in at the doctor's clinic to meet up with a Gideon Bryant."

"I've heard of him. He's related to the doctor's wife." A flush of heat ran through Claire. "The *other* doctor. Bryan's younger brother."

Marcus raised a brow at her, looking like he might ask more.

Better change the subject. "Are your things outside?"

"My trunk and bag are at my new house." Marcus leaned back in his chair like a proud papa.

"They gave you a house with the deal?" This was almost too much to take in. It's like Marcus had taken on a different life while she was away. "Where?"

He nodded toward the door. "One street over and a little farther north. Close to the church."

"And you went there before coming to tell us you were in town?" Claire propped her hands on her hips.

"Just dropped my stuff and asked the first stranger I saw where to find the two prettiest gals in town." He drank a swig of his coffee, then set the mug back on the table with a *clunk*. "'Course when I got to that saloon he sent me to, I found a better way to ask directions. Eventually, someone told me how to find the two of you." That self-satisfied twinkle in his eyes was all too familiar.

"Marcus." All she could do was shake her head.

Claire was pouring coffee for a table full of miners that evening when Marcus came in with Gram on his arm. That tall profile with the broad shoulders sent her heart into a leap of joy. It was better than the Fourth of July to see him.

"You two come sit right here." She motioned at the special table in the corner where she usually put Gram.

Marcus glanced at it, and his forehead creased. "Mr. and Mrs. Bryant said they would come have supper with us. And maybe the doctor, too."

Claire's stomach flipped. Bryan was coming. "Why don't we pull this other table next to it?" She scooted the two together, so there were enough seats for six.

Once Marcus and Gram were settled, she poured coffee in their mugs. "We're having goulash and cornbread tonight. Lilly makes it better than Mama. Wait 'til you taste."

"Your Mama's an excellent cook," Gram piped up, her mouth coming to rest in a pinch.

Claire's gaze flicked to Marcus, and he met it with a smirk. "I know, Gram. You taught her well. I think you'll like Lilly's stew too, though."

The front door opened, and Miriam Donaghue walked in, an infant swaddled in the crook of her arm. An elegant woman trailed her, brown hair coifed under a fashionable hat that matched her dusky blue day gown. Behind them entered a tall, dark-haired man Claire hadn't met, followed by Doc Alex.

Marcus rose as the group strolled toward them. "Mr. and Mrs. Bryant. Doctor and Mrs. Donaghue. So glad you could all join us."

Miriam stepped forward. "It's a pleasure, sir. Claire, I'm so glad you're here too. I've been dying for you to meet Leah. And look at my niece, Emily. Have you seen such a precious angel?" She paused for only a breath to beam at the sleeping face in her arms, then glanced up again. "Leah, this is Mrs. Malmgren's granddaughter and Marcus's sister, Claire Sullivan. She's beautiful, isn't she? And just as sweet as she is pretty."

The heat that flooded Claire's face made her duck and take a step back. "I'm not... I mean..." She forced herself to meet Leah's gaze. "It's a pleasure to meet you, Mrs. Bryant."

The group settled into seats, and Claire poured coffee for each. Where was Bryan? His family and close friends were all here, so surely he would have made an effort to join them. Had a patient come in with an emergency? Did she dare ask? Maybe if she found the right opportunity.

Claire escaped to the kitchen while Marcus peppered the men with questions about the town. Barely a minute later, she was back out with a tray full of steaming soup bowls.

"Mmm... Lilly's goulash smells wonderful," Leah said as Claire positioned a bowl in front of her. "Thank you, Miss Sullivan. You're lucky, Miri. You have access to food that you don't have to cook any time you want."

Miriam sank back in her chair, as far away from the soup as she could without making it obvious. Her face had paled and took on a greenish hue.

Claire rested a hand on her shoulder and leaned close, as if admiring the babe in her lap. "Shall I bring you something different to eat?" she whispered.

Miriam turned weak eyes on her. "No. Thanks. I'm not quite myself tonight, but I'll be fine." Her glance shot to her husband at the end of the table. She needn't have worried he would notice, though, as he was deep in conversation with the others. Just like a man to miss what was happening under his nose.

Claire eyed Miriam once more and saw Leah doing the same. "If you change your mind, let me know."

Before she left to check on the other patrons, Claire swept one last glance around the table. Gram seemed to be doing fine with her food. Marcus leaned close to tell a story that had her grinning. The others all had full plates and mugs. She nibbled her lip. Was now a good time to ask?

"Is there any chance you could join us, Miss Sullivan?" Doc Alex had noticed her lingering.

"Oh, no. I was..." *Just ask.* Claire squared her shoulders. "Should I bring another bowl of stew? I mean, will your brother be joining you?"

The doctor's gaze shifted toward the front window. "He hadn't returned to the clinic when we left, so I imagine he's working somewhere. We left a note for him to come here, but you never know if he'll be back in time."

"Oh." Disappointment surged over her like a bucket of cold water. At least she'd have time with Bryan tomorrow on their ride. She spun to leave, but a hand on her arm turned her back.

Miriam's pasty face held a weak smile. "If you get a chance to come by tomorrow, Claire, please do. Leah and I really want a chance to visit with you." Her chin bobbed downward. "And I want to show off this sweet one when she's awake."

Claire glanced toward Leah. The woman's mouth tipped in a gracious smile.

"Thank you. I'll come in the morning if I can." And just maybe she'd run into Bryan while she was in that part of town.

Chapter Seventeen

*C*laire had every intention of rising early the next morning, but she'd tossed for hours before finally succumbing to sleep. She forced her groggy eyes open and pushed up in the bed. The smell of coffee told her Gram must already be outside.

Marcus was coming for breakfast today, and he'd always been an early riser. She'd bet a day's wages he was sitting in the rocking chair beside Gram, sipping weak coffee and watching the sun rise.

After slipping into a dress and tying her hair back with a ribbon, Claire opened the bedroom door. A male voice drifted from the porch. Yep, Marcus.

Claire poured her own cup and stepped outside.

"G'mornin', sunshine." Marcus beamed at her from the chair. She raised a brow at him. He always had been too chipper in the morning.

Claire focused on her grandmother. "How are you today, Gram?"

"Fine, darlin'. Countin' my blessings."

"It's eggs, cooked oats, and toast for breakfast. Sound all right?" She glanced between them.

Marcus rubbed his lean stomach. "I'm ready."

Over breakfast, Marcus described his new two-bedroom home. "It's plain compared to our house in North Carolina, but it suits me." He stuffed a spoonful of oats in his mouth and followed it with half a slice of bread.

"Sounds like a palace compared to what some of these people live in." She didn't mean the comment to sound as bitter as it came out.

Marcus swallowed the bite that puffed his cheeks. "So you've met some people in town? Can you introduce me? I'd like to start getting to know the folks."

"Sure."

"Marcus." Gram's voice quivered a little. "I'd be happy to introduce you around, too, and there's someone special I want you to meet. Has Claire told you my news?"

Claire's heart thudded faster.

Marcus turned raised brows on her. "No."

Claire wrinkled her nose to return his jab. Maybe playfulness could make the news absorb more easily. Marcus was so protective, he'd never take kindly to a new man in Gram's life unless he approved of him first.

Gram reached over to pat her grandson's arm. "Marcus Timothy, I'll be gettin' married soon."

Marcus surged to his feet, his chair tumbling backward in the process. "What?"

Gram's face held a soft smile, not perturbed by his explosion. "His name is Moses Calhoun, and you're gonna love him. He's such a good man."

Turning flashing eyes on Claire, Marcus rested his fists on the table. His voice dropped a register. "What in Solomon's name is going on here?"

"Marcus, your language." Claire spoke the word as a warning. Marcus never added color to his words, and maybe she could use a scolding to distract him from his ire.

He raised a finger at her. "Don't split hairs with me. Why haven't you stopped this, Clara Lee Sullivan?"

Why hadn't *she* stopped this? Well, there was one thing she could stop here and now. Marcus had pitched his hissy fit. Time to bring him back to reality.

Claire straightened her spine and squared her shoulders. "I haven't stopped this, Marcus, because Gram is a full-grown woman, capable of making her own decisions. Mose *is* a good man, God-fearing from what I've seen. Ask any person in town. Folks around here have known him for years. And the long and short of it? *He makes Gram happy.* With those facts in his favor, I didn't see a need to put a stop to it." She leaned back and crossed her arms.

Marcus eyed her, still leaning over the table. Then he glanced at Gram. "I still don't like it."

Gram reached forward to rest her hand on his. "Moses should be back in town this week. I want you to meet him, get to know him. If you can see your way to it, I'd like you to marry us, Marcus. But if you don't feel comfortable with it, I understand."

Marcus sucked in a quick breath. He didn't speak for several moments as he stared at her. "I'll think about it." He slipped his hand over Gram's. "I better get going now. Thanks for the breakfast." Then he nodded to Claire and strode toward the door.

As it closed behind him, Gram's chest shook in a chuckle.

"What are you laughing at?" Of all the emotions Gram could be feeling, laughter was the very last she expected.

The lines around Gram's mouth formed a lively grin. "Oh, I suppose that went better than I anticipated."

Claire hoisted the stacked crates of bread onto one hip so she could unlock the café's back door.

When she pushed it open, Aunt Pearl sat at the table inside slicing ham. "Hello, dearie. I told Lilly to take a day off, so it's just you and me for the lunch crowd."

Easing the crates onto the work counter, Claire turned and immersed her hands in the wash basin before she unpacked the loaves of bread. "She did look pretty worn out last night."

"That's exciting about your brother coming to town, eh? A real preacher. And you didn't say a word."

"I had no idea." Claire pulled the bread knife from its hook on the wall and started slicing a loaf. "It was as much a surprise for me. It's great that he was able to find a church right here in Gram's hometown. Pretty amazing how it all worked out."

"Looks like the Lord's hand at work to me."

Claire inhaled a breath. Why hadn't that occurred to her? "Yes, I suppose you're right." *I'm sorry for not thinking of You first, Lord.*

"Oh, I almost forgot. Doc Bryan stopped by and said he wouldn't be able to keep the meetin' this afternoon. Said he was headin' up into the mountains to birth a baby."

A knife of disappointment sliced so deep into Claire's chest, she almost had to sit down under the weight of it. "Did he say when he'd be back?"

Aunt Pearl shrugged. "Didn't say. Could easily take all night, I reckon'. There's no tellin' about these things."

Claire swallowed. "I don't suppose there is." She sat for several minutes, mindlessly slicing bread. Her whole body felt numb. But why should she let this bother her?

She had to pull herself together. Bryan hadn't planned to cancel their outing. It was simply his work that pulled him away. And if there was anything she knew about, it was the demands placed on a doctor.

But couldn't he have stopped at Gram's to tell her himself? Gram had kept her busy all morning making things for Marcus's new home, so she hadn't even been able to visit Miriam and Leah. She would have been home had he tried to find her.

Stop it, Sullivan. Give the man the benefit of the doubt. Claire straightened her shoulders. Bryan would be back in the café tomorrow, and all would be well.

Bryan didn't come into the café the next day. Or the two days after that. By Thursday evening, Claire could barely keep a smile on her face as she served dinner to the regulars. How dare the man go so far as to kiss her, then just walk away? She should have known better. Should have seen this coming.

And why was she letting his absence bother her so? She knew better than to let any man get to her.

The bell on the café door jingled, and her head jerked up. An infuriating reaction. The man who stepped into the dining room was familiar, but her heart still plummeted. Doc Alex. His features were close enough to Bryan's to know they were brothers, but Alex's face was a bit more refined, more playful, with a shock of straight dark hair that brushed across his forehead. Bryan's masculine features spoke of strength, his eyes a silent intensity, especially when they shone green against his auburn hair.

Alex stopped in front of her, and Claire motioned toward an empty table. "Welcome to Aunt Pearl's. Have a seat, and I'll start you off with coffee."

He gripped the brim of his hat. "Actually, I need to take food home with me. Three plates if you have them."

Claire nodded. "Certainly. Just three?"

Alex's mouth formed a thin line. "Yep. Gideon and Leah took the wee one back up on the mountain this morning, so Miri's stuck with just Bryan and me." He raised a rueful brow. "Not such great company. Might be why she's feeling poorly." His forehead formed twin creases. "I hope it's nothing more. I thought dinner from the café would be a nice surprise."

Claire tried to smile. "I'm sure it will." Although if Miriam's illness was from the cause she suspected, food may not help much.

She wrapped up three plates for the doctor, forcing her mind not to dwell on the fact that Bryan would be eating with them. Why didn't he just come into the café? Should she ask Alex if he was all right?

When she handed him the bundle of food, Alex smiled. "Much obliged."

"Tell Miriam I'll be by to check on her tomorrow. I'm so sorry I haven't come sooner. Things have been busy helping Marcus settle in and keeping up with the baking for the café." She motioned toward the kitchen.

"She'll be thrilled whenever you get to come." Alex turned toward the door.

This was her last chance. "Uh, doctor?"

He twisted back. "Yes, ma'am?"

How to ask it? "Is your brother… I mean, is Doc Bryan all right? He hasn't been in to the café in a while, so I wondered..." She let her voice drift away. What exactly did she wonder? If he was healthy? If he cared about her at all?

Alex snapped his fingers. "That's right. He told me earlier to tell you he has to make rounds on the mountains for the next couple days. He'll see you later this week." He held up the bundle of food. "He's been working long hours lately. Probably won't get in to eat this until long past bedtime, but I'll leave it for him anyway. Don't know why he does it exactly. There weren't any emergencies that I know of. He's just out making rounds. It's like he's determined to prove something." He shrugged, a sadness clouding his features. "I haven't figured out if he's trying to prove it to others or to himself."

As she watched the man walk away, a cold weight settled in Claire's chest. Of course. She should have seen it from that very first day, when he was so exhausted he couldn't find the energy to be civil. He worked himself into the ground, but something drove him. Was it to help others? Certainly, but the shadow that so often cloaked his mood pointed to a deeper ache. But what?

With everything in her, she wanted to help this man. How could she do it?

Bryan trudged down Elm Street, weariness weighting every one of his bones. Jackson at the livery had already retired for the night, so it'd taken extra minutes to wipe down Cloud and settle him in his stall. The horse deserved it though, after their long excursion into the mountains.

As Bryan passed the street that held the café, his eyes drew toward that building, just three doors down from the corner. Light shone through the windows, sending out a cheery radiance. Inviting. Claire would be in there. Everything in him wanted to turn and approach the glow. Find Claire. Take her in his arms and make up for these last days he'd stayed away.

He clenched his fists, forcing his feet to walk straight on Elm. Claire needed time with her brother. The way her face had lit, hanging on every word the man said. She obviously adored him. And why not? From just those first few minutes, it'd been clear Marcus was charming and held a deep affection for his baby sister.

He released a long breath. He was tired. Tired of working so hard—for so little success. Tired of playing second fiddle to charming young men. Not just with Claire. All his life with Alex. As much as he loved his brother, couldn't he have just one person who liked Bryan better? Without him having to work his soul away to earn it? Was that really too much to ask?

Bryan yanked open the door to the clinic, then slammed it shut behind him. Stomping down the hallway to the private chamber he occupied alone, he tossed his doctor's bag on the ladder-back chair by the door. His eyes scanned the room. This room he'd lived in for two years now, first with Alex, and now very much alone.

The same four walls. Same wash basin with his shaving kit laid out. The chest of drawers beside it. Two trunks now filled the gap where Alex's bed had stood. And that was it. The extent of his home. Sparse was a kind word for it. Drab. Colorless.

Lonely.

His mind drifted to Claire. She brought so much life and vibrancy everywhere she went. At the café, the customers adored her. In her grandmother's home, the place seemed to come alive with her presence.

His eyes took in his meager surroundings again. What would she think of this place? Think him too boring to waste time with? Bryan sank onto the bed and stretched out, boots, sweaty shirt, and all. He let his eyes drift closed, scrubbing a hand over his face. He didn't care anymore. Wouldn't care. He was too tired. Tired of working so hard. Tired of being judged and found lacking.

Chapter Eighteen

*C*laire pressed the rolling pin into the dough for the cinnamon rolls, even as her eyes wandered to the window. Six days since she'd seen Bryan. What was he doing? What was he thinking? What had she done to scare him off?

Alex said he wasn't sick, just working too hard. What made him push himself so? She pressed harder on the rolling pin, then wrinkled her nose when the dough split. She tossed the wooden cylinder aside and balled the dough in her fists. If Bryan didn't show up at the café tonight, she was going to find him. She wanted answers.

The thump of boots sounded on the porch outside, and Claire whirled, still clutching the lump of dough. Bryan?

A knock sounded on the door. Her heart catapulted in her chest, and her feet lunged forward. He'd finally come. Just as Claire touched the handle, a voice outside called a greeting.

"Good afternoon, ladies. It's Ol' Mose back in town."

The stab of disappointment was stronger than any knife in her chest. Claire sank against the wooden divider, her weight pressing on the knob. Not Bryan. She fought down the burn in her throat, tears stinging behind her eyes. *Get it together, Sullivan.*

She squeezed her eyes shut, inhaling a long breath. As it filled her lungs, she forced her mind to focus on the kindly man waiting on the other side of the door. *Smile.* She raised her eyelids, then stepped back and pulled the door open.

"Woowee, Miz Claire. It's awful good ta see you." Ol' Mose stood on the porch, hat clutched across his chest.

"Thank you, sir. Won't you come in?" She stepped to the side and swept a hand for him to enter. "Gram's napping, but you're welcome to cinnamon rolls and coffee until she wakes."

He glanced around the room, then shot her a toothy grin. "Can't say as I'd pass that up. Thank ye."

As Mose settled in a chair at the table, Claire pulled out a plate and scooped two rolls onto it. Should she wake Gram or let her finish the nap? He would have to get used to adjusting his schedule to fit Gram's needs, so might as well let him start now.

"How was your trip?" She set the plate and mug in front of him, then moved back to the dough she'd been working with before his arrival.

"Smooth an' steady." He sipped the brew, then released a long sigh. "That's the best coffee I've had in weeks."

"Thank you. I'm not sure if you've heard, but my brother Marcus is in town. He's the new preacher." She eyed the man out of the corner of her eye.

He dropped both hands to the table and leaned forward, twisting to look at her with one of his grins. "No foolin'? That's the best news I've heard all day."

A smile pulled at Claire's face. "We're pretty excited."

He took another sip of the coffee, still half turned in his chair. "A preacher in Butte again. Thank the Lord." He mumbled the words. "And it's our Marcus. Who'da thought?"

Boots sounded on the porch outside, and Claire's heart jumped into her throat. Bryan? The knob turned, and the door pushed open as a familiar profile filled the door. Marcus. She gripped the edge of the work counter as she bit her lip against the disappointment pressing down. Would Bryan ever come?

"Hello." Marcus's voice held a strong note of caution as he eyed Ol' Mose at the table.

The older man stood and stepped around the table, hand extended. "Howdy."

Claire wiped her hands on her apron and scurried to join the men, preparing to act as a buffer if necessary. "Mr. Calhoun, I'd like you to meet my brother, Marcus Sullivan. Marcus, this is Gram's…" Friend? Fiancé? No word seemed right. "This is Mr. Calhoun."

"Jest call me Ol' Mose like everyone else does." Mose gave his usual charming grin as they shook hands, but Marcus seemed to be armoring himself against its effects.

"I've heard of you."

"Marcus, come sit down for a sweet roll and coffee." Claire gripped her brother's elbow and tugged. Where was Gram when she needed her?

Her brother acquiesced, moving stiffly to his usual chair, across from the one Ol' Mose had occupied.

While Claire prepared another plate for Marcus, she kept an ear tuned to every nuance of sound from the men.

"So tell me about yourself." Marcus's voice was deeper than usual, like an overprotective Pa vetting a suitor for his daughter.

"Well, let's see. Spent my younger days a'trappin', back when trappin' was big time. Worked with the best of 'em, too. Jedediah Smith, Jim Clyman, Hugh Glass, an' a couple others ye might notta hear'd tell of."

Claire had never heard of any of them, but she kept that to herself. She placed the plate of cinnamon rolls in front of Marcus. He acknowledged it with a single nod, not taking his eyes off Ol' Mose.

"Trapped fer a lotta years, then sold my snares an' bought Zeke an' Zeb an' the wagon. Been seein' the countryside ever since, runnin' freight between Butte, Helena, an' Fort Benton."

The bedroom door opened, halting Marcus's reply as all three of them turned to look. Gram appeared, her hair arranged nicely, not the usually bed-rumpled look after her nap. She must have heard the male voices.

"Mose is here, Gram, and Marcus, too," Claire called. From the smile that touched Gram's lips, she was pretty sure Gram picked up on the undertone in her voice.

"My two favorite men in all the world." Gram extended a hand as she stepped toward the table.

Both men stood as Gram approached, and Ol' Mose strode forward to take her outstretched hand. "Darlin', you're a sight for sore eyes." He raised the fingers to his lips, and Gram's smile bloomed in full color.

Claire tried to catch Marcus's eye, but he studied the pair intently. His brow wrinkled, and he looked as if he were trying to comprehend every word, every nuance between them. It wasn't the wary, guarded expression from before. This one looked like he was trying his best to understand. Poor Marcus.

"Gram, come sit and have cinnamon rolls with the men." Claire turned to prepare yet another plate. She might as well be at the café for all the serving she was doing.

As the three sat and visited, Gram maneuvered the conversation well, asking Ol' Mose questions that gave him opportunities to share tidbits about himself. By the end of a quarter hour, Claire felt like she'd known the man for years, and she had a better inkling of why everyone who knew him thought so highly of him.

Claire glanced out the window, where afternoon shadows seemed to be taking over. It was almost time for her to be at the café, and this last batch of cinnamon rolls still needed to rise and bake. She nibbled her lip as she turned to face the threesome at the table.

Marcus caught her look. "What's wrong, baby sister?"

"I need to leave for the café, but it'll be another hour before these rolls are finished. Gram, could you put them in the oven in half an hour? I'll come back to get them after they've baked."

"Of course, darlin'." Gram waved a hand. "I'm jest sorry I slept so long and made you do all the bakin' today."

"How's about we bring the rolls to ya when they're ready?" Ol' Mose spoke up.

The weight rolled from Claire's shoulders. "That would be wonderful."

An hour later, Claire was working beside Lilly in the café's kitchen when the knock sounded on the back door.

"I'll get it." She stepped back from the work counter where she'd been slicing zucchini and wiped her damp hands on her apron.

When she pulled open the door, the smiling couple stood at the base of the step. Ol' Mose held out two stacked pans of cinnamon rolls, covered with a cloth. "Special delivery fer ya, ma'am."

Warmth surged through her chest. "Bring them on in. Would you two like to eat dinner while you're here?"

"Thank ye, dear, but I told Moses I'd fix a special dinner for him tonight." Gram reached out a hand. "Come here, though, Clara Lee. I want to tell you something."

Claire slipped past Mose as he brought in the rolls, then took Gram's hand and descended the single stair.

Gram pulled her several steps away. "Marcus stayed around for a while to get to know my Moses." She spoke in a conspiratorial whisper. "They seemed to be getting along pretty well. Marcus agreed to marry us in his new church."

"Oh, Gram. That's great." Claire pushed aside the emotions warring in her chest and squeezed Gram's hand. "I really am happy you've found someone special. Do you have a date planned for the ceremony?"

A grin spread across Gram's face. "Sunday after the first service."

Claire inhaled so quickly, the breath caught in her throat, and coughs doubled her over.

Gram patted her back as Claire struggled to catch her breath. Finally she straightened, wheezing to pull air into her lungs.

"You all right, darlin'?"

Claire swallowed, blinking away the moisture in her eyes. "You're getting married Sunday? As in, day after tomorrow?"

"That's our plan. There's not really a reason to wait, is there?"

"Um…You don't think you're rushing into it a bit?"

Gram's hand found Claire's while her other arm slipped around Claire's shoulders to pull her into a sideways hug. "I've been thinkin' about this a while now, Clara Lee. I'm not rushin' into anything. I don't know how many days I'll have left, so best not dawdle once I make my mind up. Besides, honey, you'll be wantin' to get back home and on with the rest of your life. I don't want you to feel obligated."

Tears choked Claire's throat, so she couldn't respond right away. "Gram, I *want* to be here." It was all she could manage.

Gram only squeezed her hand.

What in the great state of Georgia was she going to do now?

Claire carried the coffee pot toward the café's kitchen as she pondered her options. She couldn't stay at Gram's house after the wedding. Not with newlyweds and only one bedroom. She blinked that thought away before images began to form.

Maybe Marcus's new home? It had two bed chambers and needed a woman's touch as bad as Marcus needed his next meal.

"Miss?"

Something touched her elbow as the word registered. Claire whirled to face the source. A tall, homely man sitting at one of the café tables jerked back. She forced a smile onto her face. "Yes, sir?"

What little she could see of his face above the beard flushed red. "I'm...uh...just wanted more coffee. Please." He scooted his mug forward, then his chin dipped like a turtle retreating in its shell.

Remorse pricked her chest. "Of, course." As she poured the brew, the bell on the door clanged, jerking Claire's attention up.

The familiar face of Miriam Donaghue sent a surge through her. She yanked the coffee pot up as the liquid reached the top of the mug, used her apron to swipe at the drops she'd spilled, and almost ran to greet the Donaghues.

Miriam. Doc Alex.

Her heart plummeted as he turned to shut the door. Where was Bryan?

Claire swallowed, trying to force down her disappointment so she could paste on a smile. *Lord, I need your strength.*

"Claire, how are you?" Miriam reached for her and pulled her into a hug, coffee pot and all.

Claire breathed in the scent of roses, closing her eyes to savor the embrace. "It's good to see you."

After several moments, Miriam drew back and held Claire's shoulders at arm's length. Her brows drew together, forming twin lines between them. "Are you feeling all right?" One side of her mouth pulled. "You look as pale as I feel. But the circles under your eyes are worse than mine. What's wrong?"

Claire had to turn away or the sting of tears would give her away completely. "I'm fine. Just busy." She forced cheeriness in her voice as she pointed to an empty table. "Would you like to sit here?"

The burn of Miriam's gaze followed her as Claire poured coffee in the two empty mugs and Alex assisted his wife with her chair.

Claire kept her head down. "I'll be back soon with your food." She turned and fled to the kitchen.

Behind the curtain, Claire clunked the pitcher on the table and bent over it, gulping in steadying breaths. This was her chance to ask about Bryan. And she could *not* cry when she spoke the question.

"Are you all right?" Lilly's voice pulled Claire's attention, and she looked up to find the woman's dark eyes brimming with concern.

"Yes."

Aunt Pearl swept through the curtain, saving Claire from having to say anything else.

"Lilly, I have a group of six. Hungry as vultures."

The younger woman turned back to the stove and scooped food onto plates.

Claire straightened from the table. "And I need two plates when you can, Lilly. No rush." Because it'd take several minutes before she'd work up the nerve to face Miriam again.

Lilly was overly efficient, though. Too soon, she slid two plates of pork and pickled cabbage across the table toward Claire. "Is there more you need?"

Claire swallowed. "No. Thank you."

As she approached the table where the Donaghues sat, Miriam glanced up, a smile spreading across her face. "Thanks, Claire."

Inhaling a breath, she forced her mouth to open. "How are you both?"

Miriam looked up to catch Claire's gaze. "Much better now, thanks." Her eyes flicked toward her husband, and her head gave the slightest of shakes.

Had she still not told her husband the news?

Claire bit back a nervous smile. Miriam already had a glow shimmering from her face. The secret didn't seem to bother her, but what was she waiting for?

Miriam looked to her husband. "Do you think we should take Bryan a plate?"

Claire's nerves did a flip in her stomach.

Alex shrugged. "Probably. Doubt he'll eat otherwise."

"Is he okay?" There. She'd asked. But now she couldn't breathe as she waited for the answer.

Miriam's mouth twisted. "There's nothing medically wrong with him, if that's what you mean. He's been working like a fiend, though." She sank back in her chair. "Hasn't come in before ten any night this week. If no one calls for him, he goes out to check on people that are perfectly fine." The hint of sarcasm in her voice was laced with affection.

Alex chucked. "He's just a bit hard-headed. But that's not one of the official maladies we learned in medical school."

Anger burned through Claire, sparking in her gut and flaming as it rose upward. Relief that he was healthy did little to slow the fire. He was avoiding her on purpose. Working himself sick so he wouldn't have to see her. Well, too bad. When he finally came back from hiding out for the day, she'd be there waiting.

And she would get some answers.

Chapter Nineteen

*C*laire didn't move from her place in the shadows by the clinic door as the weary figure trudged toward her on the street. Watching the outline of his slumped shoulders and drooping head made her chest ache. She wanted to reach out and stroke away whatever was bothering him. Pull him into a hug. Take on all his worries.

She straightened her spine as he slogged up the steps. She'd come here for answers. And answers she would have. Squaring her shoulders, she stepped out of the shadow, into the moonlight streaming onto the boardwalk.

"Bryan."

His head jerked up. "Claire?" The word rasped, as though he'd drug it across a rocky desert.

"Bryan, what's wrong?" That wasn't what she'd planned to say, but the sight of him so dejected, the desolation in his voice. It reached into her chest and squeezed until she ached.

She kept her feet planted, though. Refused to take another step toward him, lest she fly into his arms.

"What are you doing here?" He seemed to have gathered himself from that moment of raw emotion. His voice was distant now. Wary.

Claire propped her hands on her hips. "I came for answers. I want to know why you've been avoiding me. Is it something I did?" She hardened her tone. "Or is kiss-and-run your usual way of getting to know your patients." That might have been a low blow, but she had to know how he'd react. His true colors.

Bryan's head whipped up, wide eyes picking up a glimmer from the moonlight. His nostrils flared. "No. Claire, I thought you wanted time with your brother. I was giving you space."

She fought to close her dropped jaw. "Space? Why in the city of Jerusalem would I need that?" She took a step forward, peering up to see his face better.

An emotion flashed across his features. Pain? "I... You...you seemed so happy to see him. I didn't think he'd want me around."

That was the most preposterous thing she'd heard in months. Claire dropped her hands to her sides. "Did you ever think maybe I'd want you around? And Marcus too. You don't think he'd want to get to know you?"

Bryan shrugged, his hands finding his pockets. "Why would he? He came here to see you and your grandmother. I'm no one to him."

Claire took another step forward, bringing them less than two feet apart. But she kept her hands at her sides. "How could you say that? Even if you meant nothing to me, Marcus would still enjoy your company. The two of you are so much alike. You both care so much about people." She thought of her crazy brother. "He's a little reckless sometimes, but I think you'd like him if you gave him a chance."

He raised his chin. "Gave *him* a chance? He could have come to see me if he'd wanted."

She lifted her brows. "Really? Cause I had to wait 'til long after any decent hour to find you tonight." Dare she say what she really wanted? He might not like it, but someone had to speak the truth.

"You know what your problem is, Bryan Donaghue?"

He tilted his chin, eyeing her. "What?"

Ire rushed through her veins. "You work too hard. And not just long days helping patients."

She poked a finger at his chest and took a tiny step closer. "You work too hard to make people like you. You try to *earn* their respect and friendship, when all it would take is to let them see the real you." She smoothed her hand over his heart. "The you I've seen."

He gripped her wrist, holding her hand in place. The rapid beat of his pulse thumped through her palm.

"I don't know how to do that." His words were soft. Achingly sincere. "It's different with you. You accept me even when I have nothing left to give."

She stretched her other hand up to rest on his shoulder, a smile tugging her lips. "You mean I don't put up with your sass."

A crooked grin touched his face. "You bring it out in me."

That grin started the familiar flutterings in her stomach. Her gaze wandered up and fell into the depths of his. The earnestness there took her breath away.

He brought her fingers to his lips and pressed a warm kiss on her knuckles. "I've missed you."

He could have knocked her over with a breath, but she couldn't resist a bit of teasing. "You could have fooled me."

His gaze narrowed, and he slipped a hand around her waist, pulling her closer. "Very sure."

His mouth lowered to hers, and the touch was ecstasy. So soft. So rich. His hand came up to caress her cheek.

The kiss ended far too soon, and Bryan pulled back a few inches. She forced her eyes open.

He watched her. "Claire." His voice came out breathy, but still so rich.

Her heart answered him. No words needed. She touched the stubble on his cheek, the rough texture awakening the nerves in her fingers.

"Can I take you and your grandmother to church tomorrow?" His voice was husky now. "I hear we have a fine new preacher. One I'd like to get to know."

The way his lips quirked. She couldn't resist raising on her toes to plant a soft kiss. "I'd love to. But Gram's already spoken for."

He didn't let the kiss fade, but swooped back down for another. His lips strong on hers. Mama had once said, *never decide whether you're in love when you're with the man. Wait to pray about it when you're apart.* But if she could judge by how she felt at this moment, she would admit she was falling so quickly for this man. He was so good. And kind. The way he cared for others. Even the way he was so hard on himself. And he was such a good kisser.

They were both breathing hard as he pulled away and rested his forehead on hers. "I better get you home. You shouldn't have come here by yourself." He caressed her cheek.

"I had to."

With a groan he pulled back, pushing himself away from her, then dropping his hands to his sides. "Let's go before I lose the last of my senses."

The cool night air rushed over her skin where his touch had been. Claire gripped her arms across herself.

He motioned for her to precede him down the steps. As they strolled the moonlit street, he kept himself at least a foot away.

"So did you say Gram's spoken for tomorrow? Is Ol' Mose back?"

"You could say that."

He picked up on the dry tone in her voice, giving her a sideways glance. "Meaning?"

"They're getting married after the service."

Bryan pulled up short. "Tomorrow?"

She pursed her lips. At least she wasn't the only one shocked. "Gram says she wants to make good use of what days she has left."

He *harrumphed* and kicked at the ground. "She's hardly ready to keel over." He ambled forward, staring at the ground as his brow furrowed. "So what are you going to do now?"

A knot formed in Claire's stomach. "I...haven't decided yet." She'd been trying not to think about it. And tonight wasn't the time she planned to start. Tomorrow. After the wedding would be soon enough. "Ol' Mose is coming for breakfast in the morning before we walk over. Will you come too?" She watched him out of the corner of her eye.

"Will Marcus be there?"

She wrinkled her nose. "Said he has too much to do getting the church ready. Even though we've already spit-shined the place."

They were in front of Gram's house now, and Bryan held out his hand at the base of the steps. She slipped her hand into his, warmth sweeping up her arm.

At the top, he turned her to face him. "That's too bad. I was hoping I'd have a chance to talk with him. I hear we have a lot in common."

"Be here at eight then." She reached up and kissed his cheek. "Goodnight, Bryan."

His "goodnight" followed her inside.

Claire settled into the pew between Gram and Bryan. There couldn't have ever been a day as glorious as this one. From the first rays of the fiery sunrise this morning, she'd had the feeling it would be a new beginning.

As Marcus strode up the center aisle to the front of the church, the set of his broad shoulders sent a rush of pride through her chest. He'd done it. The goal he'd worked so hard for. Her brother had his very own church in this wonderful town.

Standing behind the little pedestal where his Bible rested, Marcus looked out over the crowd. The room was full to capacity, and some men stood along the back wall. Sunday was the one day the mines didn't run, and even Aunt Pearl had closed down the café to mark this grand occasion.

"I can't tell you what an honor it is to stand before you all. Many of you I've met over the last week, and you can bet I'll be getting' to know each of you. I'll want to hear your stories. What brought you to the place you're in. So for now…" He clapped a hand over his chest. "I'll share a bit of mine."

Marcus went on to tell about his own road to salvation. How he'd accepted Christ as a boy of seven, then spent the next eight years trying to earn his way to heaven.

As Claire listened to the tale she'd heard before, a thought crystalized in her mind. Marcus's story could almost be Bryan's if you changed the ages a bit. Bryan was still working himself weary trying to earn his way. Was it just to win the favor of others? Or God's good will, too? He'd told her about how he became a Christian as a boy. But maybe he, like Marcus, was still trying to earn his way into the free gift he'd already received.

She slipped her hand into Bryan's, lacing her fingers with his. He gave her a gentle squeeze. *Lord, help him see he already has You. Let him feel Your overwhelming love.*

"So you see, you don't have to earn God's favor. You can work your whole life to be good enough, but God wants you just as you are. Just as He made you." Marcus pushed his hands into his pockets and scanned an earnest gaze through the crowd. "For a while I felt guilty about accepting the gift. Not the kind of guilt you have when you've done something wrong, like the time I used Mama's favorite wedding quilt to build a fort after she told me not to." That got a chuckle from the crowd.

"I'm talking about false guilt. The kind you carry as an extra weight. An unnecessary burden that you just can't release." His eyes touched hers. Intentionally? "That burden of false guilt can only be released when you open yourself to the Heavenly Father and let him show you the truth. Then you can move forward clean. A new beginning."

False guilt. The words radiated through her mind. She closed her eyes, and the dreaded images flashed behind her closed lids. Mandy. Burns and raw skin covering her arms. Tears streaming down her face. The guilt crushing. She'd known Mandy's stepfather left marks when he "punished" her. The broken arm. The constant bruises. She should have said something. Should have done something. Before it was too late. Before Mandy lay in that bed, disfigured and praying for death.

A squeeze on her hand pushed against the memories. Claire forced open her eyes.

Bryan watched her, concern wrinkling his brow. "Are you okay?" He mouthed the words.

She took in a breath, then released it. Yes. She had to be okay.

She was beautiful.

Bryan never took his eyes from Claire, standing beside her grandmother as the wedding ceremony progressed. She took his breath away. The love in her gaze as she watched her grandmother take Mose's outstretched hand. She poured that same love onto everyone she met. This woman cared about people. Cared enough to take action. To give of herself to make things better for others.

He swallowed. One day, he wanted to be up there, standing across from her in the front of the church. *God, what do you think?* He let the idea settle over him as he watched Claire through the vows and the final blessing.

After Marcus presented Mr. and Mrs. Moses Calhoun to the crowd, Claire enveloped her grandmother in a hug. People surged around the newlyweds, all laughing and chattering.

Bryan stood but didn't leave his spot in the pew as he tracked each of Claire's movements. *Lord, please make Your will clear to me.*

She extracted herself from the throng of well-wishers and turned to pick her way toward him. Her gaze shone as she met his. But as she came closer, he could tell her smile was a little wobbly.

He held out an arm, and she slipped into it, pressing against his chest as he wrapped her close. There were people everywhere to watch, but he didn't care. She needed a hug. And holding this woman felt more right than anything he'd done in years.

Chapter Twenty

Bryan nodded at Marcus as the preacher joined them on the lawn about halfway through their picnic lunch. Most attendees had brought food to celebrate the happy couple, and Bryan had kept Claire close as they sat with Miriam and Alex.

"They finally let you stop to eat?" Claire eyed her brother as she sat on the blanket, propped against one hand.

"Are you kiddin'? At every blanket, they piled something new on my plate. I don't think I'll need to eat again for weeks." Marcus rubbed his stomach, then looked over at Bryan. "I like your town. Good people here."

The swell of pride took him off guard. "Thanks. They are good people. A hard-working lot."

"I reckon' we'll fit in just fine, won't we, baby sister." He gave Claire a nudge, then glanced sideways at Bryan. "When Claire was a kid, she used to do her chores, then go over to the neighbor's house and finish their chores, too. Never did know when to stop, that one."

Bryan eyed Claire. That pretty pink in her cheeks came from more than just the sunshine. "I think she's done that a few times lately, too."

She sat up straighter. "I was just doing what I was asked."

"Ha." Marcus turned to Bryan again. "She might have been a hard worker, but doing what she was told was not one of my baby sister's strong points. Hard-headed." He shook his head as if she were a hopeless case.

"Hey, now." Claire's sassy side reared its head as a twinkle lit her eyes. "At least I wasn't reckless with everything." She turned to Bryan with the same conspiratorial tone Marcus had used. "Marc couldn't look at a tree without climbing it and then jumping from the branches. He'd broken bones fifteen different times before he turned ten. I think that's why Papa became a doctor. Couldn't afford to pay someone else to fix all Marcus's injuries."

Bryan grinned. These two were quite a pair. He'd been close with Alex and their sisters, but not with quite the same devotion Claire and Marcus showed. That alone spoke volumes for her older brother's character.

Maybe it wouldn't be so bad to get to know the man.

Later that evening, Bryan stepped into the little back room off the clinic and tossed his hat on a chair back. He glanced around the drab room. So cramped compared to the great outdoors where he'd spent most of the day. If he planned to marry Claire, he'd need to start thinking about better living arrangements.

Claire's pretty face played through his mind, and Bryan sank onto his bed. She was amazing. Her kindness. The genuine way she cared about others. Her spunk. Her heart.

He dropped his face into his hands. What was he thinking? A woman like that would never think of marrying a curmudgeon like him. *God, why did You ever bring her into my life?*

God wants you just as you are. The words from Marcus's sermon rippled through his mind. God didn't want *him* the way he was. Not with all the ways he messed up. The way he got so many things wrong. Surely.

Just as He made you. The words sat for several moments in Bryan's mind before their true meaning began to blossom. God *had* made him like this. But didn't God expect him to work to improve himself? *My grace is sufficient for you. My strength is made perfect in your weakness.* The scripture Marcus had read as he closed the sermon.

Bryan scrubbed a hand over his face, then raised his eyes heavenward, past the wooden timbers lining the ceiling. "Lord, I don't know what to do with Your grace. How do I live without trying to prove myself?"

No thunderclap. No audible voice from heaven.

Bryan lit a lamp and grabbed his Bible from the shelf. Where had Marcus read that scripture? Second Corinthians, wasn't it? He flipped there quickly and scanned the pages. Finally, in chapter twelve.

And he said unto me, "My grace is sufficient for thee: for My strength is made perfect in weakness." Most gladly therefore will I rather glory in my infirmities, that the power of Christ may rest upon me.

Glory in my infirmities. Now there was a new thought. How freeing would it be to stop trying to make himself what others wanted? Instead, he could focus on doing what he truly loved. Helping patients, yes. Spending time with a lovely young lady? Absolutely.

His eyes found the passage again. "Lord, You're gonna need a lot of grace to cover my weakness. Help me lean on You. I want to." Oh, how he wanted to.

Bryan loosened his boots and lay back on the bed, clothes and all. For the first time since he could remember, the weight that pressed down on him...was gone.

Something wasn't right.

Claire pushed herself up in bed and scanned the room. Light filtered in through a window. A window?

That's right. Her breath leaked out with a whoosh. Marcus's spare bedroom. She'd officially moved in with Marcus after the wedding festivities so the newlyweds could be alone where Gram would feel most comfortable.

Hair prickled on the back of her neck. Something didn't feel right. Didn't…smell right. Then her brain came alive. *Smoke.*

She threw the covers aside and landed on the floor, running the two steps to the open window that looked out on the west side of town. Nothing unusual that she could see.

Goose prickles skittered across her arms as she dashed out of the bedroom, through the parlor area, and flung open the front door. The smell was stronger now. In the distance, a red glow hung over the eastern side of town, surrounded by a dark haze.

"Marcus!" She sprinted back to her room. "Marcus! The town's on fire! Get up!"

She threw on a skirt, not even worrying about a shirtwaist. Her nightgown was modest enough to perform the task. As she laced her work boots, the thuds sounded from Marcus tromping through the kitchen.

"I'm going to help put out the fire," he yelled. "Go check on Gram, then see if you can help the injured."

"Be careful."

But he'd already slammed the door.

Blasted boots. She only laced them halfway, then tied them off and lunged for the door herself.

At every house she passed, Claire banged on the door with all her strength. "Fire!" As soon as stirring sounded inside, she moved onto the next. They were only two streets over from Gram's, and she caught glimpses of the house every so often. The fire wasn't close yet. It still looked to be farther east. Most likely Elm Street.

Panic welled in her chest. The clinic was on Elm Street. And the café not far from it. Claire sprinted toward Gram's. She yelled as she ran. Maybe the inhabitants would hear the warning.

Leaping onto Gram's porch, she banged hard on the door. "Fire! Mose, Gram, get out! There's a fire."

It took an eternity as she fought to catch her breath, but she finally heard the bar slide away from the door, and it pulled open.

Ol' Mose was pulling up a suspender over his shirt. "Where at? Where can I help?"

She was already jogging back down the steps. "Get Gram out of town where she'll be safe. Maybe take her to the church."

Claire raised her skirts and sprinted through the alley, stopping at the café to bang on the back door. Would Aunt Pearl hear from her apartment upstairs? "Fire!"

It was only a few seconds before the door yanked open. Aunt Pearl in her usual determined focus. "Grab these pots an' bring 'em with us." She pointed to the row of cookware hanging from hooks on the wall.

Claire clutched one in each hand and another under her left arm. Aunt Pearl held the others.

Together, they hauled the equipment toward the street, heading toward Elm. When they reached the crossroads, Claire froze.

Bright red flames lit the night sky, leaping from building after building like a fiery wall. The roar of the flames filled the air. Crackling.

Her mind spun. Her chest ached, struggling to pull in breaths. Images. Flames. Skin ravaged by the fire.

A hand gripped her arm.

She screamed, jerking backward.

"Claire!" The yell sounded just louder than the noise of the fire.

She forced open her eyes.

Miriam gave her arm a tug. She leaned closer to be heard. "We're taking the wounded to the grassy area by the church. Can you help spread the word, then meet us there?"

Claire nodded, forcing herself to inhale deep gulps of the smoky air. She had to slow her racing heart. "Are Bryan and Alex both safe?"

"Alex is moving the injured. I think Bryan might be with him." Miriam gave her arm another squeeze. "Be careful."

As her friend jogged away, Claire took in the sight one more time. She forced her eyes not to focus on the flame. *Wounded.* They would need bandages and medicine. The fire was consuming the building next to the clinic. An office of sorts. It didn't look like the clinic had been touched yet. She sprinted toward it.

At least she could see for herself that Bryan was out.

When she opened the front door, the air was thick and hazy. Dark. She fumbled forward, leaving the door open to allow in moonlight. She'd only been in here that one time with Gram, but she followed the wall toward where she hoped was the hallway.

"Bryan?"

No answer, but she found the door to the examination room. Good. When she pushed it open, light streamed in through the window. A breakfront along the right wall housed all manner of medicines and bandages. She grabbed empty wooden crates from a stack in the corner and started filling them from the cabinet.

"Bryan!"

Still no reply. *Thank you, Lord.* He'd probably been one of the first helping to put out the fire or clearing victims from their homes. He was the kind of person who would disregard his own safety to help others. Such a good man.

A cough sounded from another part of the clinic. She froze, her heartbeat accelerating again. Surely she'd heard the sound wrong. It had to be noise from the fire outside. Buildings falling or something.

She dropped the crate on the floor and surged toward the door.

"Bryan!" She screamed his name. Still no reply. Was he lying unconscious?

The smoke was much thicker in the hallway now. Had the fire reached the clinic already? She felt along the walls on both sides. With the darkness and the thick smoke, she couldn't even see her extended hands. Was this what

Gram felt like since she'd lost her sight? Never sure what lay around her? Unnerving was an understatement.

She touched a door on her right, found the latch, and pushed it open. "Bryan!"

Still no answer. With light from the window, this looked like a smaller examination room. A cot rested on the far wall. No one inside.

Where was Bryan? Maybe that cough had been her imagination. Her mind playing tricks. Still. She had to know for sure.

Her nerves wound in knots, and she moved back to the hallway. Her fingers brushed a door on the other side. Pushing it open, hot, acrid outside air rushed in. Must be the back exit.

"Bryan!"

No more doors until she found one at the end of the hall. The handle almost burned her fingers. Hands shaking, she used her skirt to protect her as she turned the knob.

Smoke billowed from the room, blasting Claire in the face. "Bryan!" Coughs caught her, bending her over with their intensity.

Raising her outer skirt to cover her nose and mouth, she forced her way in. Bright red lit the far room. Fire. Moonlight shone through gaps around the leaping flames.

She forced herself to spin around. Couldn't let the fire paralyze her.

Moving as quickly as she dared, she felt her way along the wall, almost tripping over a chair by the door. Empty space next. Then her toe caught on…a bed.

Her eyes were adjusting to the dim light now. Either that or there were more flames giving off light. Heat radiated on her back through the cotton of her nightshirt.

She ran her fingers along the quilt covering the bed. They struck something. Solid, but not hard. Cloth.

"Bryan?"

A moan sounded from the bed.

Chapter Twenty- One

"*B*ryan!" She reached toward his head. Gripped a shoulder. Shook it. "Bryan, you have to get up. Fire!"

Another groan.

Oh, God. I've never needed you more than I do now. Please *help me get him out of here.*

She shook him again, then felt for his arms. He lay on his side, facing away from her. She rolled him on his back, then pulled him up to a sitting position, using her whole body for strength.

"I'm up." The mumbled words were barely distinguishable. He was conscious? *Thank you, Lord.*

"We have to get out of here, Bryan. Can you stand?"

No response.

She pushed his feet to the floor. He was in his stockings, but at least he felt fully clothed. "Can you stand?"

Still no answer.

She looped his arm around her neck like Papa used to do with their neighbor when he'd drunk too much at the tavern to walk home on his own.

"Stand up." Her sharp command must have gotten through, because he made an effort to rise. She finally got him on his feet, but he leaned so hard to the side, he pulled her down. Before she could find some leverage, he'd fallen back on the bed, dragging her almost on top of him.

That wasn't going to work.

The flame was mere feet away now, spreading along the walls at least a foot per minute. "God, help me!"

She turned back to Bryan again. She gripped his wrists and pulled him up to a sitting position, then turned and looped his arms over both her shoulders, like she was carrying him piggy back.

"Stand up!" With the noise of the fire so close, he might not have heard her, but she could feel him pushing up as she pulled him to a standing position.

The smoke pressed down hard on her chest. She needed to cough, but she'd lose all balance with Bryan's weight on her back.

Bent half over, she pushed forward in the direction she'd come. Bryan's feet moved too. At least she wasn't completely dragging him.

She teetered under the weight, but her shoulder struck the door frame, helping her regain some balance. They were through the door now, Claire pushed forward blindly down the hall until a glimmer of moonlight indicated the back door.

Almost there.

With the last bit of strength she had, Claire stumbled forward several strides into the grassy area behind the clinic.

Then she collapsed, allowing Bryan to roll off her back as she landed on the ground beside him. Coughs overtook her, and she rose up on her knees as her body wracked. Pains shot through her chest with each cough, and finally, she sank back to the ground.

She had to get aid. Had to help Bryan. Every part of her body craved rest, but she couldn't collapse until Bryan was cared for.

Glancing back at the building, she could see the red flames leaping in the sky on the other side of the roof. The first priority was getting Bryan farther away from the building.

Pushing herself up, Claire stumbled around the side of the clinic farthest from the fire. Men swarmed the street just a little ways down. Some had formed a line, passing buckets between them. She ran that direction.

"Help!" She grabbed the arm of the largest of the men in the line. "Bryan was in the clinic. He's hurt."

Without a word, he broke from the line and jogged after her. Claire lifted her skirts and ran as fast as she could. She stumbled several times and would have gone down had the man not grabbed her elbow.

At last they reached Bryan, still crumbled on the ground. "Get him away from the fire."

The man scooped Bryan up, tossing him over his shoulder like a sack of flour, then jogged in the direction of the church.

Claire fought back a protest against the way Bryan was being carried. His hands clutched the man's shirt, which meant he must be awake. *Lord, please don't let him die.*

She snagged the arm of another young man they passed. "Inside the clinic. In the first treatment room, there's a box of bandages and medicine. Get everything out you can and bring them to the grass by the church."

"Yes, ma'am."

As the fellow trotted away, she scurried to catch up with Bryan's helper. Her chest ached, but she kept running.

Her mind scanned its recesses for everything she knew about how to treat smoke inhalation. The main thing was to make sure his breathing was unobstructed. *Lord, please don't let him be burnt.* The old images of her childhood friend tried to resurface, but she pushed them back.

A crowd had started mingling in the grass beside the church. The man lowered Bryan to the ground, and Claire rushed forward to cradle his lolling head as he fell back.

There were enough lanterns around that she got her first good look at him. A sob caught in her throat.

Bryan's face was swollen and soot-darkened. She reached out, afraid to touch him. How much pain must he be in? Her chest ached.

His breathing was ragged, but he *was* breathing. His eyes were closed. The way his head had dangled, had he slipped unconscious? She had to help him.

Raising her head, Claire scanned the area. People seemed clustered in groups, all murmuring in low voices. Was Doc Alex here? That's who she needed.

She rose and strode through the crowd. "Alex?" she called out in a low voice. Hopefully she wouldn't disturb the injured, but she had to find Bryan's brother.

"Here."

The familiar voice sent a rush of relief through her. Claire spun and ran toward him. "Bryan's hurt. He was in the clinic, and I barely got him out. His face is swollen, but he's breathing. He's not conscious."

Alex started in the direction she'd come. "Where is he?"

They wove back through the huddled people. When they were about fifteen feet away, she pointed to Bryan, still lying on the grass where she'd left him.

Alex ran forward and crouched by his brother. He placed two fingers at Bryan's neck to check his pulse. Then he knelt down to press his ear to his chest. Alex closed his eyes as he listened.

Claire couldn't breathe herself as she watched and waited for a prognosis.

Alex raised back up and touched Bryan's swollen face. "How you feelin' there, big brother?" His voice cracked on the first word. From the smoke or emotion?

A groan sounded as Bryan's eyelids flickered, then opened to small cracks. "Rather...be...dead." His voice was so hoarse it was barely audible. But he'd spoken.

Claire couldn't contain herself any longer. She dropped to her knees on Bryan's other side. Taking his hand, she cradled it in both of hers. "I'm so glad you're alive."

He turned his head slightly to look at her. "Me...too." His eyes drifted shut, and he squeezed her hand. A light pressure, but the message was strong.

She leaned forward and pressed a kiss to his forehead, near the hairline where he wasn't as swollen. No matter that Alex was watching.

She looked up at the younger doctor. "Is it okay if I find water to wash his face?"

Alex had a funny expression, but he nodded. "That would be good."

Men had brought over barrels of water, and the women of the town had brought blankets and cloth to use as bandages. The man she'd ordered to gather supplies from the clinic was just arriving with a helper, and they placed the crates with the other supplies.

She pressed a hand to the man's arm. "Make sure only Doc Alex disperses these. All right?"

The man nodded. "Yes'm."

The last thing Alex needed were the remnants of his supplies passed through the crowds. Especially when the people may not know which tonic to use for which ailment.

With a basin of water and cloth in hand, Claire wound her way back to the doctors. She resumed her place beside Bryan, then glanced up at his younger brother. "They brought several crates of supplies from the clinic. They're over by the water barrels, but I told the men not to allow anyone to use them except you."

Doc Alex rose. "I'll see if there's anything I can give Bryan for the pain or to help him breathe, then I need to get back to the others. I'll have Miriam come over when she can."

Claire forced a competent smile, but it was probably more of a grimace. "I know there are a lot of people who need help. I'll let you know if we need anything."

Wringing the water from the cloth, Claire focused on Bryan's face as she smoothed the damp fabric over it. The soot wiped away easily enough, and his face wasn't as swollen as she'd first thought.

His breathing was steady now, though still rough and raspy. Was he awake?

She dipped the cloth back in the water, squeezed the excess from it, and then wiped Bryan's forehead again.

A tiny shadow of a smile curved the corners of his mouth. "Feels...good." He struggled with the words, and a coughing fit overtook him.

Claire reached under his shoulders and helped him turn on his side to help with the coughs.

He seemed to be gagging for a moment, then a thick, dark substance spewed from his mouth. He sank back against the ground, a trail of the dark liquid leaking down the side of his jaw. The effort seemed to have drained the last of his strength.

Claire wiped his face, her chest aching at the sight. Was he going to make it? The thought petrified her, feeding a fear that threatened to overwhelm. She pressed her eyes shut.

God, touch his body. Heal him. Please. I can't lose Bryan, too.

A warm hand touched her knee, resting there.

Claire opened her eyes and stared at Bryan's strong hand, thick auburn hairs brushing its surface. Even with the agony he was suffering, he still thought of her. The idea clenched her chest tighter.

She raised her gaze to watch his face. So much pain played across his features. The loud rasp of his breathing so labored. Could she trust God with his life? Truly relinquish her fears? Would God heal him? Did God care about Bryan as much as she did?

For I know the thoughts that I think toward you, saith the Lord, thoughts of peace, and not of evil, to give you an expected end. Then shall ye call upon Me, and ye shall go and pray unto Me, and I will hearken unto you.

The words from Jeremiah filled her mind. One of Marcus's favorite passages. He'd even written the Scripture in the letter he'd sent from school as she was preparing to travel to Butte. *Pray unto Me, and I will hearken unto you.*

She stared up into the night sky. Smoke from the fire snuffed out the stars, but the moon still glimmered through the haze. "Lord, will you please heal Bryan?"

For the first time that night, as the prayer lifted from her lips, it took with it the shroud of fear over her heart. She inhaled a deep breath and released it, peace settling into her soul. *Thank you, Father.*

Chapter Twenty-Two

*C*laire stayed with Bryan for the next several hours, offering him sips of water each time he awoke. Helping him roll over when he coughed up the sooty phlegm. Stroking his hair and soothing him as he slept. With each quarter hour, the love inside her grew stronger. She may not have known him long—less than two months—but her soul connected with this man beyond what she'd ever thought possible. If God chose to heal him—and she prayed constantly for God's healing—this was where she wanted to spend the rest of her life. By this man's side. Helping and supporting him in whatever role God assigned.

Every time worry threatened her peace, Claire raised another prayer toward heaven.

The night sky was lightening now. Dawn would be on them soon. This night couldn't end soon enough.

Claire sat with her hands clasped around her knees, watching the minimal activity in the clearing. News had come a half hour ago that the fire was out. All the wounded were in this gathering, under the watchful care of Alex, Miriam, and a horde of exhausted townspeople. Most were resting now, worn out from the long night behind them.

"You should...lay down." Bryan's hoarse voice sounded beside her.

She glanced at him. His eyes were more alert than they had been since the fire.

"Rest."

Tenderness surged through her as she reached to stroke his shoulder. "I'm okay, love. It's almost morning."

He raised a hand to finger the cloth at her elbow. "I'm sorry...you've had...to take care of me."

Just like this man to put others before him. She took his hand from her arm and raised it to cup her cheek. "I'm glad I finally have a chance to spend time with you."

The smallest hint of a smile touched his mouth. "Me, too."

After a moment, he looked around on the ground. "Is there...water?"

She took up the canteen and slipped a hand behind his head to help him drink.

He was able to swallow more than a sip this time, drinking several gulps before he pulled away.

As she replaced the cork, he struggled to rise. "Wait. Lie still, Bryan. Rest."

He didn't rest, though. "Help," he grunted as he strained. The man was hard-headed.

She helped pull him to a sitting position, then slipped an arm behind his back for support.

He tugged her other arm. "Sit beside me."

She eyed him warily. His color seemed better now, or maybe that was the effects of the dawning light. The swelling had almost left his face, though his lips were still a bright red.

She slowly eased in beside him. Bryan slipped his arm around her, but a coughing fit caught him, and he turned away. The sounds and the way it wracked his body hurt her own chest.

When it finally subsided, Bryan took another gulp of the water, then replaced the cork and eased out a long breath. "What a night. Haven't felt this bad since…never."

He slipped his arm behind her again, and Claire settled into him, turning to see his face. "I'm just thankful you're alive."

He squeezed her waist. "Me, too."

They sat for several minutes like that. The silence was wonderful. Everything was wonderful, just having him next to her.

At last he spoke. "How did I get out? Do you know?"

She eyed him. He didn't remember? "I carried you."

He raised both brows. "You?" His hand gave her waist a little pinch. "I don't believe it." And from his teasing tone, it sounded like he really didn't.

She straightened her spine. "I did."

He studied her eyes for a long moment. "You pulled me out of the clinic? Out of the fire?"

She swallowed. He knew her fear. Knew what it had taken for her to go toward the fire. She could only nod.

He grazed the side of her arm with his finger, sending a skitter of bumps across her skin. "Can you tell me about it? Your experience…with fire?"

He didn't say fear, but they might as well call it what it was. "My fear?"

A nod was his only response, his eyes not wavering from hers.

She inhaled a breath. She needed to tell him about it. *Lord, this will take Your strength.* With the prayer on her heart, she opened her mouth and began her story.

Bryan listened without a word as she told about her early years playing with Mandy. How they'd built their own playhouse in the woods, climbed trees, followed Marcus around. She told him about the way they loved to stretch out on the grass in the pasture to enjoy the sunshine.

And then she told about the bruises that always covered Mandy's arms. About the broken arm. The broken fingers. The burns on her palms. How afraid Mandy was of her stepfather. How Mandy would scarcely breathe the few times Claire saw her around him. And finally, that awful day when Mandy fell into the fireplace.

"Mama said Mr. Steinberg swore it was an accident. Mandy had been ladling soup from the pot hanging over the fire and lost her balance. He'd been drinking that night, though. Mandy had seen him with the bottles of his homebrewed liquor and was afraid to go home. She was more afraid of him missing her though. I wanted to say something to Mama and Papa, but I knew I'd be tattling.

Mama hates anything that looks like gossip, and I was afraid she'd wash my mouth with lye."

The shame washed over her anew. Because she'd been worried about punishment, her friend lost her life.

False guilt. Marcus's words from the sermon came back to her. She pressed her eyes shut. Had the guilt she'd struggled under all these years been of her own making?

Bryan's fingers brushed her arm again. "Did you see her…with the burns?"

Claire inhaled a long, shaky breath as the images rushed in. "Yes."

His other arm came around her, encasing her in the strong shelter of his grip. Claire burrowed. She was supposed to care for his wounds. Be strong for him.

But as a sob escaped, she clutched his shirt and allowed the tears to fall.

Bryan held Claire in his arms, brushing from her face the hair that escaped her braid. The wrenching sobs tearing through her were enough to shatter the last bit of reservations he had about this woman. He loved her. More than he could ever imagine loving a person. And her tears were breaking his heart.

She needed it, though. Mum had always said tears were cleansing for a woman, and from the sound of it, she was wiping clean the slate of fear and guilt she'd carried since she was a five-year-old child.

After minutes—or hours—her sobs faded to shudders. He never loosened his grip, even though his chest ached like the fire still raged inside of it. A little bit of physical pain was nothing compared to the struggles Claire had been through. Who would let a five-year-old child see the burns that killed her friend? That kind of damage would have disfigured the girl, probably beyond recognition.

He tightened his hold. *God, bring her peace.*

At last she pulled back, wiping her eyes with her sleeve. "I'm sorry, Bryan. I didn't mean to do that."

He took her chin in his fingers, pulling it up so she looked at him with those red, puffy eyes. "I'm glad you did." He hated the hoarse scratching of his voice, but it didn't seem to bother her. "Thanks for telling me your story."

She offered a weak smile. "It's a cautionary tale."

So much came clear to him now. Why she hated any hint of a bully. Why she poured so much of herself out for others. That was her nature, too, but she did it like she was driven. Was she trying to pay some kind of penance?

He pulled her head against his chest. "It wasn't your fault, you know. It was his."

She stiffened, then released a shuddering breath. "I think I'm beginning to see that. It's hard, though. Changing everything I've held onto."

For better or worse, that fear and guilt had been part of what shaped her. He fingered a lock of hair. "You know what your problem is? You work too hard."

A shaky chuckle shook her shoulders. "Seems I've heard that before."

He allowed his fingertips to brush her neck. "It was good advice."

Silence took over for several more minutes. It was more than enough just to hold her.

She pointed toward the sky. "Look."

His gaze followed her finger to a display of fiery splendor only heaven could create. "It's beautiful." Too perfect for words.

"The only kind of fire I've been able to tolerate is the sky with the rising and setting sun. It's not as majestic in North Carolina as it is here though." Her words were wistful. An undercurrent of longing. Was she thinking about going back to Carolina? Over his dead body. But there would be a better time and way to tell her.

For now, he pulled her closer. "You know what the fire in the sunrise represents, don't you?"

She turned a questioning gaze on him. "What?"

"A new beginning."

Two days later, Bryan heaved a piece of charred wood onto a stack of debris piled high. All around him, men called to each other and grunted from their labors. The town had come together in remarkable ways to help those who'd suffered from the fire. Basically, starting at one end of the damage and working their way to the other, clearing out anything that couldn't be salvaged. The flames had affected at least a third of the buildings in Butte proper.

His chest still ached, and his voice rasped more than he'd like. But at least he could work for an hour or two at a time before he had to stop and rest.

"Good to see you out, Doctor."

Bryan turned to see Martin Daly, mine owner extraordinaire, with his shirt sleeves rolled up. He didn't look very soiled, but still. At least he wasn't hiding behind his front door while the rest of the town worked.

He nodded at the man. "Good to be out."

"I heard you got caught in the fire and we almost lost you."

Bryan nodded again. Martin wasn't one for small talk, so there must be a reason for this. Bryan wished he'd get to it.

"I'm glad we didn't lose you. You're a good man, Donaghue. This town needs more men like you."

The words struck Bryan in his chest. *The town needs more men like you.* And this from Martin Daly, one of the most influential men in town. A man who'd shown pretty good judgement, from what Bryan had seen. He swallowed, trying to gather his wits. "Thank you, sir."

Martin glanced at the debris from the washhouse Bryan was helping to clear. "I've been thinking about what you said about my men and their lung sickness." His gaze lifted to Bryan's. "I'd like to talk more about purchasing some masks. Maybe a larger trial. Fifty or so, to make sure they're the right approach."

Bryan forced his gaping mouth to close. "That…that sounds good, sir. I've placed an order for twenty more, but I'll send word to up the count to fifty. I really do think they'll make a difference, but a larger test is a good idea. Make sure we're not missing something important." He was prattling on, but the excitement beating in his chest made it hard not to.

"Sounds like a plan. I'll cover the cost of all fifty." Martin stepped forward and extended a hand.

Bryan glanced at his own, his palm solid black from soot.

"It's all right, man. You're fine as you are." Martin spoke quietly.

Bryan raised his gaze to meet the man's eyes. Respect shimmered there. He reached out and clasped Daly's hand, gripping it solidly. "Thank you, sir."

"All right then." Martin stepped back. "I'm off to negotiate with Lanyard. Trying to get the old coot to provide some of the necessities at his cost for the families whose homes were wiped out. He's a tough cookie, that one. Doesn't give things away well." His mouth twisted in a sardonic smirk.

"Good luck."

Bryan watched Martin pick his way around piles of burnt timbers as he headed back to the street. Had that really happened? Martin was willing to pay for a trial of fifty, then possibly for all his mine workers? *Lord, it's too good to be true.*

You're fine as you are. Had Martin meant that? Or was he simply saying he didn't mind getting soot on his hands?

For man looketh on the outward appearance, but the Lord looketh on the heart. The scripture he'd read that morning came back to him. Daly's respect would be nice, but it really didn't matter. God saw Bryan's heart.

Footsteps sounded behind him, daintier than the men clomping across the boards. Bryan turned to a sight that cranked up his heart rate. He let a slow grin spread across his face. "You're the best picture I've seen all day."

Claire smiled at his words, ducking her chin as pink flushed her cheeks. "You're not so bad yourself."

And right there in front of half the town, she stepped closer and planted a kiss on his lips. It was a chaste kiss, to be sure, but scandalous nonetheless. A few whistles and calls sounded from around them, but Bryan ignored it all.

He didn't hold back his grin, though. "You better watch it, or I might ask you to repeat that. And you'll get more than you bargained for."

The pink in her cheeks turned bright red. This woman was beyond perfect. A combination of sassy and pure innocence.

She held up a bucket of water and a ladle. "Would you like a drink?"

He took the ladle and scooped it. "Is this a service you're offering to all the men?"

She raised a pert brow. "Of course. I'm not stingy with my help."

A chuckle rumbled in his chest, almost bringing on a coughing fit before he stopped it. "I guess that's all right. I wouldn't love you as much if you were."

The impudent expression softened into sweet tenderness. "It's mutual."

That sealed his decision. Enough waiting around. It was time to claim this woman as his. Although, she'd pretty much just done that with the kiss in plain view. Now it was his turn.

He squared his shoulders. "Are you busy tonight, Claire?"

Confusion clouded her gaze as she cocked her head against the sun. "We...um...Just helping Aunt Pearl."

"Can you ask off for tonight?"

A smile played at the corners of her mouth. "I guess. Can I tell her the reason?"

"I need you." And that was the honest truth. But probably not the way she would take it.

She inhaled a breath. "All right then. What time should I be at the clinic?"

Always trying to help. That was his Claire. He tapped her button nose. "I'll pick you up from Marcus's. Six o'clock all right?"

"Fine." She gave him another curious glance.

She wasn't getting another word from him on the matter, though. He stepped closer and lowered his mouth for a touch on her lips. "You'd better share the water with the others, or they'll mutiny."

Chapter Twenty-Three

Claire studied the dresses laid out on her bed. The gray polished muslin with lace frills on the sleeves and bodice? If they would be working around the fire-ravaged areas, that was definitely not the right dress. But a relaxed dinner at the café? It would be perfect.

The yellow calico was a much better fit for working around the fire, with its frayed edges and chemical stains on the skirt from working in papa's clinic. But nothing about it was flattering, and it certainly wasn't appropriate for an evening spent with a suitor.

So what exactly were their plans for the night? Bryan had been so cryptic. And for some crazy reason, she hadn't asked for details.

At last she settled for a beige shirtwaist with layers of flounces on the sleeves and a becoming cut at the waist. With her forest green skirt, it was somewhat elegant, yet still practical. She sighed. It didn't matter if she had to wear flour sacks, as long as she was spending the evening with Bryan, but it would still be nice to turn his head a little.

The knock sounded just as she inserted the last hair pin in her coif. The loose curls tumbling from the knot wouldn't hold if the work Bryan had planned was too strenuous. But she'd deal with that if the time came.

Through the thin walls, she heard Marcus open the front door. The men's greetings drifted in as she stepped back for a final glance in the mirror. Tilted her head. Not her best effort, but it would have to do.

"Clara Lee, Bryan's here." Marcus's voice boomed from the next room as if she were completely deaf. As if the walls weren't the thickness of a single plank, transmitting the sound with little barrier.

"I'm coming, dear brother." A little too much honey dripped from her tone, but he'd get the point. No matter how much she told him to lower his voice, the boy couldn't do it.

As she stepped into the parlor area, Claire's gaze found Bryan instantly. He was magnificent. Not only did his plaid waistcoat pick up the green tint of his eyes and the string tie at his neck accentuate its strength and thickness, but he actually wore a jacket with wide lapels, unbuttoned though it was.

She'd never seen him in anything other than waistcoat and shirt-sleeves, usually rolled at that. Her simple shirtwaist and skirt were pauper's clothes compared to the way he'd turned out.

"I, um, need to go back and change." She whirled to escape.

"Wait."

The word stopped her in her tracks. She slowly turned back as Bryan took two long strides across the room. He clasped her hand and held it out as he looked her over. Admiration shimmered in his eyes when his gaze met hers. Poor man. Either he was still regaining his faculties from the fire, or he'd been gone from fashionable society for far too long.

"You're beautiful, Claire. Stay just like you are." He raised her hand to his lips but turned it over at the last minute and pressed a kiss to the fleshy part at the base of her palm.

Merciful heavens. Bumps skittered up her arm.

"A-hem." Marcus cleared his throat from behind them. "You two, uh, need an escort tonight?" He placed particular emphasis on the word *escort*. Was that red creeping into Bryan's cheeks?

He turned to face Marcus, though not loosing his grip on Claire's hand. She twisted it so she could lace her fingers through his.

Bryan's voice was genial as he answered. "We'll be fine, but you're welcome to come if you'd like."

Oh, gravy. The last thing she needed was Marcus sitting between her and Bryan, the third wheel telling childhood stories she'd rather forget.

"We'll be fine." She strode toward the door, pulling Bryan behind her and sending Marcus a sweet smile. "Aunt Pearl said she'd save a seat for you tonight."

Marcus raised a brow at her but didn't move to follow.

They strolled along the streets of Butte, heading north toward the outer edge of town. Bryan filled her in on his conversation with Mr. Daly, one of the mine owners he'd met with about the masks. Her heart soared at the outcome.

"Bryan, that's wonderful." She slipped her hand into the crook of his arm. "*You're* wonderful. You've done it, you know. Finally brought about change for the miners."

He ducked his chin, brows lowering as he kicked the ground. "It's a start, but we've a long way to go still."

True, but they'd get it done. She had no doubt.

"How are you feeling today?"

He raised his head, giving her an off-kilter smile. "Ready for Miriam and Alex to stop fussing over me."

She rolled her eyes. "You almost died in a fire. Let them fuss for a few days. I might do my share of it, too."

His gaze darkened as he stared squarely into her eyes. "That, I might allow."

Heat flamed up her neck, and she looked away. Maybe they should stick to a lighter subject for now. "Has Miriam finished cleaning and reorganizing what didn't burn at the clinic?"

The men had been able to stop the fire midway through the smaller examination room, so the main treatment room and the waiting area were still intact, along with the supplies Claire hadn't dumped into crates the night of the fire.

"She wouldn't stop until she had it completely spotless." He gave her a dry smile. "My sister-in-law's nothing if not hard-working."

Claire chuckled. "She fits in the family then."

They were nearing the church now, the trampled grass on the far side another reminder of that awful night. "When do you think you'll start rebuilding your room off the clinic? Or will you stay with Miriam and Alex?"

"No, no." He gave a hearty shake of his head. "The newlyweds need their space." He cast a sideways glance at her. "And room for expansion, too."

Claire studied him. "Do you mean…?"

He nodded.

A grin pulled her face. "She finally told. I couldn't figure out why she was keeping it a secret so long."

His brows pulled close. "You knew?"

She gave him a patient look. "It was hard not to notice if you watched her try to eat a meal. Poor thing was miserable."

Bryan pursed his lips and shook his head. "I completely missed it. Alex didn't say anything either."

Probably best to let that one go. "So when do you start rebuilding?"

A funny look took over his expression. "I was thinking to start tomorrow. At least with the planning and ordering of materials."

What did his expression mean? Part uncertainty. Part question. Part eagerness. They reached the grass beside the church, the undisturbed side, and he motioned for her to step off the street.

"Do I get to know where we're going?" She kept a teasing tone in her voice, but his secrecy was killing her.

"Just right around there." He motioned toward the back of the church.

When they turned the corner, Claire pulled to a stop. A blanket was spread across the grass, held down by a basket, jar of purple flowers, and a canteen.

"I hoped we could have a quiet dinner. There's something I need your help with." Bryan's voice rumbled in her ear as he stood right behind her.

"I'd love to." It was perfect.

After they settled on the blanket, Claire unpacked the food from the basket. Fried chicken, cobs of corn, sourdough bread and jam, and her favorite, cinnamon sweet rolls for dessert. "Is there a chance I made any of this?" she joked as she loaded a plate for him.

He chuckled. "It's possible. Everyone knows Aunt Pearl serves the best food around."

She sank back on the blanket and sampled the sweet roll first. "I don't usually stop to eat these, but I love them." The gooey sweetness exploded on her tongue, and she closed her eyes to savor the flavors. Cinnamon, of course. A touch of nutmeg. Honey. Her favorites.

When she opened her eyes, Bryan was watching her. "If you ever enjoyed my company half as much as that cinnamon roll, I'd be the happiest man alive."

She raised a brow, fighting an embarrassed grin. "Who says I don't?"

His green eyes darkened, but he didn't move closer. Instead, he took in a deep breath and met her gaze. "Claire, I'm not good with words, so I'm just going to say this. Will you marry me? I know we haven't known each other that long, but I already love you more than I ever thought possible."

Her breath stopped. Had he just…? The words caught her so off guard. From enjoying a cinnamon roll to *will you marry me* in less than ten seconds.

And then her wits caught up with her. Bryan just asked her to marry him. *Oh, Lord, You are truly good.* She pushed her plate aside, wiped cinnamon icing from her fingers, and rose up on her knees. She leaned forward and pressed a kiss to Bryan's lips.

He didn't seem startled this time, like he had earlier when she'd bussed him in front of all the others. That had been shamefully improper, but it had seemed like a good idea at the time.

Now, he gripped her sides and pulled her closer, sitting her almost in his lap as he claimed her lips with intensity. Blood rushed through her, warming every part of her core. This man loved her.

Far too soon, Bryan eased her back, his breath coming in ragged jerks.

She pressed a hand to his chest. "Are you all right? Did that hurt?" Why had she done such a crazy thing when the man could barely breathe on his own?

He stroked a loose curl from her cheek. "I'm all right. But we better save the rest of that for a time when we're not so...alone." One side of his mouth crooked. "Was that a yes?"

She settled back into her spot on the blanket and took up her plate. Then, with a pert glance up at him, she said, "I suppose so."

"Good." His grin was wide as he pulled his own plate onto his lap, but his breathing still wasn't steady. She'd have to do a better job watching him the rest of the evening. Alex had said symptoms could worsen several days after the fire.

"So you asked about rebuilding the clinic."

She looked up at the drawl in his tone.

"I was thinking we should look at house plans tomorrow, if you have a few minutes."

Claire straightened. House plans? She tried to keep her smile from spreading too wide. "You're not building the room on the side of the clinic?"

"Is that what you want?" He looked doubtful.

She nibbled her lip. "I guess I hadn't thought about it." She had tried not to think in any detailed terms about a future with Bryan in case he never asked her. But now...

"Well *I've* thought about it. I was thinking it would be nice to have a separate house, like Alex and Miriam. If there's room, we can put it on that empty tract between the clinic and the law office." His brow wrinkled. "I might be able to purchase the land where the office was, if Turner's willing to sell."

He met her gaze. "Would you like that? Or would you rather be closer to your Gram or Marcus?"

Her chest might as well split open from the joy swelling there. "Gram has Ol' Mose now, and they aren't likely to be home much anyway if they keep hauling freight. The same for Marcus, really. He sleeps at his house but spends every waking moment out visiting people. He might as well come visit us, too."

A thought struck her, and she fingered a pleat in her skirt. "Bryan, do you think you could ask Marcus for my hand?" She braved a look up at him. "Since Papa's not here for you to talk to him." Would he think her petty? "It would mean a lot."

"He said it was fine with him, but that if you said yes, I should write your father, and he'd put in a good word for me." A twinkle flickered in Bryan's eyes.

"You already asked?" Of course he had. Why had she doubted?

"Yes, my love." He set aside his plate and moved closer, sitting beside her. "Why do you think he didn't tag along tonight?"

"I should have known." Claire sank back against Bryan's shoulder, and they stared up at the mountain peaks surrounding them. The evening sky was beginning its array of colors as the sun slid behind the horizon. Crimson, orange, and vibrant purple.

Bryan wrapped both arms around her waist, and she rested her hands on his.

"You know, maybe we should build out here, where we can see the sunsets better." His deep voice resonated through her back. Most of the rasp he'd picked up from inhaling the smoke was gone, leaving behind that baritone she loved.

"I'd love that. Sunrises, too. Gram told me once that when Grandpop asked where she wanted to live, she said it didn't matter. As long as she could see the sun rise over the mountains each morning."

He settled his chin on her hair. "That works for me."

They sat there as the colors shifted. She'd be content to stay like that for the rest of her life. The orange melted into a fiery red at the base of a peak, closest to the sun, and a thought brought a smile to Claire's lips.

"What is it?" He touched a kiss to the top of her head.

"You know what I like most about fire?"

"What?" His tone held amused curiosity.

"Fire brings new beginnings."

Epilogue

*C*laire smoothed the ivory silk of her gown, pressing down the butterflies in her stomach at the same time. She'd been waiting three long months for this day. It didn't seem possible for it to have finally arrived.

"Nervous?"

She glanced up at her father. His smile was so much like Marcus's, enough of a teasing glimmer to put her at ease. Usually. "It's just hard to believe the day's here. Finally."

He took her hand and squeezed it. "Your Mama and I came as soon as we got all your letters. I have to say I was concerned when I read Bryan's, mildly amused when I read Marcus's, but the minute I read yours, Mama and I packed our bags and took the fastest steamer here. I knew I had to meet the man who'd stolen my baby girl's heart."

His voice cracked on the last words, and Claire stepped forward and wrapped him in a hug. "Thank you."

She couldn't say more, or she'd be crying before she ever walked into the church.

The ripple of the pianoforte sounded through the church doors, and Claire pulled back, inhaling a deep breath. She looked up into Papa's eyes. "I guess it's time."

His gaze held a sheen of moisture, but he smiled through it, extending his elbow to her. "I suppose so."

She took his arm, and they waited for the change in music. How wonderful that Gideon and Leah had sent for a piano—an exquisite McPhail pianoforte at that. And who would have ever thought Lilly would prove such an accomplished pianist? There was more to that woman than Claire had ferreted out, but as their friendship grew, she'd learn more.

The beginning notes to the bridal march sounded, and Papa pushed open the church door. As her eyes adjusted to the dimmer lighting, Claire found Bryan at the front of the room.

His gaze never wavered from her, but she wasn't close enough to read his expression.

Even as they neared, she still couldn't quite interpret what she saw in his eyes. Love, certainly, but there was more.

When Marcus asked who gave her in marriage, Papa placed her gloved hand in Bryan's. His grip was strong, sure. As they turned to face Marcus, Bryan ran his thumb across the back of her hand, a small smile tipping his mouth.

Pleasure washed through her. She was finally marrying this man.

The words of the ceremony sank deeply into her, and she locked them away to treasure for days to come. There was nothing more she wanted than to love, cherish, honor, and obey Bryan. And together, they would do the same with God.

When Marcus finally released him, Bryan gave her more than the peck on the lips that she'd expected in front of her parents and half the population of Butte. She deserved it, though, for embarrassing him that day after the fire. And the red that probably stained her cheeks was the only part of it she regretted.

Mama and the other women had put together a small feast on the church lawn, and Claire was able to maneuver it so that she and Bryan ate on a blanket positioned almost exactly where he had proposed. Marcus had plans to build tables and chairs for the church, so events like this wouldn't always require blankets on the grass. But she wouldn't have traded it this time for anything.

After Bryan helped her lower herself to the blanket, it took several moments to straighten the mass of her skirts. This had been Mama's wedding gown, and a few modifications made it fit Claire perfectly. The style was classic, and even had a short lace train in the back.

When she looked up, Bryan had both brows raised and the corners of his mouth tipped up. "Like this spot, do you?"

She raised her chin. "Very much."

He leaned forward for a quick kiss. "Me, too."

Over the course of the next hour, they had a steady stream of visitors to their little blanket. Townsfolk offering their best wishes as they passed to and from the food tables.

Every one of them knew and loved Bryan, but after a while, his foot started to tap against the blanket. Poor man.

When they had a few seconds to themselves, Claire leaned closer and murmured. "You know what I'd like to do?"

He raised his brows. "What?"

"See our new home."

His face lit. They'd carefully worked out a floor plan together, but when it came time for the actual building, he'd not let her get past the front porch. "You ready?"

"Past ready."

Bryan helped her to her feet, which was a challenge to do without tearing the lace on her gown. "I have a buggy parked in front."

A buggy? Jackson's livery had sustained quite a bit of damage in the fire, losing most of his inventory of wagons.

They said their goodbyes, Claire giving more hugs than handshakes. Mama was crying as they embraced, and Claire made the hug quick so her own tears didn't break loose. "I'll see you both when we return from the wedding trip. You'll still be here, right?"

She pulled back as Mama nodded, sniffing. "We're going to stay for another month at least and help Marcus get some things done around the church."

"Good. I'll see you in two weeks." She kissed her mother's cheek, then turned to allow Bryan to assist her into the buggy.

They waved goodbye as Bryan steered the horse onto the road, then Claire slipped her hand into the crook of his arm and snuggled close.

She breathed in a deep breath of the fall air and relaxed into the quiet. The house came into sight within minutes. "I like where you positioned it at the end of Elm Street. We get a good view of the mountains, but we're still close to the clinic."

Bryan grinned as he jumped down from the seat, then reached up to assist her. "Wait til you see the views from inside."

He held her hand as they mounted the two steps to the porch. At the top, he stopped her, then slipped his hand behind her back. "I think there's a custom we have to follow here."

Bryan lifted her into his arms like she weighed less than a child, and Claire slipped her hands around his neck.

Inside, he placed her feet on the sturdy wooden floor, but kept his arm about her waist. Claire pressed into him as she took in the surroundings. The walls were painted beadboard. A long hallway down the center led to arched doorways on both sides. "Bryan, it's beautiful. And so big." She spun to face him. "How did you build this in so short a time?"

One side of his mouth quirked. "At one point, I was thankful your parents hadn't arrived yet, so I'd have more time to finish it." He squeezed her side. "But not for any other reason."

He followed as she explored the parlor, the kitchen with its separate dining room, and a spare bed chamber. He pointed toward a closed door.

"I'll show you that room in a few minutes. It's ours." He grinned, his eyes darkening as he said the words. "I want you to see something else first, but I did want to tell you the bedroom has windows to the east, so we can watch the sun rise in the mornings."

Claire's stomach started flips again. Their bedroom. She was torn between running back out the front door and pulling him closer for a kiss.

"Come on." He took her hand, eliminating both choices, and led her back to the kitchen. He walked through, opened another door, and led her out onto a back porch.

The warmth of the evening sun soothed as Claire scanned the area. "Oh, Bryan, I love it." He'd placed two rocking chairs against the house and built a rail around the outer edge of the porch.

"We can see the sunsets from here." He motioned toward the horizon where the brilliant color palette was already forming.

Claire stepped to the rail and rested against it, breathing in the peace and wonder of this new home. Their home.

Bryan stepped up behind her, slipped his arms around her waist, and rested his chin on her head. "Here's to a new beginning, Mrs. Donaghue."

Did you enjoy this book? I hope so!
Would you take a quick minute to leave a review?
http://www.amazon.com/dp/B00WH8RBPA
It doesn't have to be long. Just a sentence or two
telling what you liked about the story!

About the Author

Misty M. Beller writes romantic mountain stories, set on the 1800s frontier and woven with the truth of God's love.

She was raised on a farm in South Carolina, so her Southern roots run deep. Growing up, her family was close, and they continue to keep that priority today. Her husband and children now add another dimension to her life, keeping her both grounded and crazy.

God has placed a desire in Misty's heart to combine her love for Christian fiction and the simpler ranch life, writing historical novels that display God's abundant love through the twists and turns in the lives of her characters.

Sign up for e-mail updates when future books are available!
www.MistyMBeller.com

Made in the USA
Columbia, SC
19 September 2020